Edward Capern

# Ballads and Songs

Anatiposi

**Edward Capern**

# Ballads and Songs

Reprint of the original.

1st Edition 2023 | ISBN: 978-3-38230-411-9

Anatiposi Verlag is an imprint of Outlook Verlagsgesellschaft mbH.

Verlag (Publisher): Outlook Verlag GmbH, Zeilweg 44, 60439 Frankfurt, Deutschland
Vertretungsberechtigt (Authorized to represent): E. Roepke, Zeilweg 44, 60439 Frankfurt, Deutschland
Druck (Print): Books on Demand GmbH, In de Tarpen 42, 22848 Norderstedt, Deutschland

# BALLADS AND SONGS.

BY EDWARD CAPERN,

RURAL POSTMAN OF BIDEFORD, DEVON.

AUTHOR OF "POEMS."

"I sing just as the bird may sing
That lives within the tree;
The songs that from my bosom spring
Are rich reward to me."—GOETHE.

LONDON:

W. KENT & CO. (LATE D. BOGUE), 86, FLEET STREET.

MDCCCLIX.

TO

MISS ANGELA BURDETT COUTTS,

A LADY

WHO WILL EVER BE REMEMBERED FOR HER

LARGE-HEARTED BENEVOLENCE,

This Volume

IS, BY PERMISSION, RESPECTFULLY INSCRIBED.

EDWARD CAPERN.

# PREFACE.

It is not without some misgivings that the Author sends forth this second volume to the public. He knows that much of the favour with which his first Poems were received, was due to a kindly sense of the difficulties under which they had been composed; and he is well aware that, in the present instance, he has less of that favour to expect; that his work will be judged purely on its own merits, and that it is not the Postman, but the Poet, whom critics will now review. Had he merely consulted his own wishes, this volume would not have appeared so soon. He had conceived the idea of writing, and, indeed, had already commenced, a larger and more ambitious poem. Many of his friends, however, were pressing in their demands for another volume of Lyrics. The time which he could devote to poetical composition was, from the nature of his daily occupation, necessarily very limited; and he has now only to hope that those who have encouraged him to write, will not be disappointed with what he has written.

In the following pages will be found many rustic songs. The Author is desirous that these should be judged *as* songs, originally written to be sung rather than to be read. Their style is homely, for their subjects are so. He has endeavoured to illustrate that singing element which still lingers in the northern district of his native county; and amply has he been rewarded for his labour of love. Written generally to simple melodies of his own, he has had the delight of hearing them sung, in many a cottage, by some of those village maidens whose charms he has endeavoured to celebrate. A Devonshire man, and proud of his birth in that beautiful county, he has found most of his subjects in the district where he resides. He has stood by the stone near which tradition states that Hubba fell; he has seen the window from which "Kitty Lile of Clovelly" held out her signal; he has talked to the old "Stone-breaker" at his work.

Whether his poems deal with sorrow or joy, they have ever been written under the influence of sincere emotion. He has sought that no word of his should tend to foment class jealousies; and, whilst singing of the sorrows and the trials of the poor, he has never forgotten how many men there are who, prosperous themselves, sympathise with such sorrows as much as he.

Lastly, he has a pleasant task to perform before he takes leave of his readers. He has to thank critics, both for their kindness and their candour; friends—scattered over many parts of the world—for generous sympathy and kind appreciation. Specially, he has to thank one dear friend—the friend who introduced his first volume to the public, and whose friendship is all the more valued by the writer that, whilst it has known no diminution of activity and sincerity from the hour when it was first bestowed upon him, that hour was one when his heart was sad, his prospects dark, and his name almost unknown.

EDWARD CAPERN.

BIDEFORD,
*Nov. 18th*, 1858.

# NOTICE.

Eight pages, which formed the additions to the previous reprint of "Poems," are now printed in this volume of "Ballads and Songs," and the volume of Poems restored to its original size. This became necessary, as many purchasers of the first edition expressed a wish to have a complete copy of the whole.

# CONTENTS.

# POEMS.

## INTRODUCTORY.

MUSING as I march along
To the numbers of my song,
Every bird throughout the dale
Warbles a melodious tale.
Pipes the thrush in merry mood,
Poet-laureate of the wood,
Far up in the topmost spray,
Loud and long his roundelay.
Then the linnet swells his throat,
While the robin tunes his note,
And the finches find employ
In the general gush of joy.
Rapt I leave the woodland choir,
Chanting to my rustic lyre,
"Do not minor minstrels sing
Sweetly with the forest king?
So may my untutored lay
Swell the music of the day."

## MY FAIRY FRIENDS.

A POET lonely? No, indeed!
Whilst nature rears her simplest weed,
And bird or insect tunes the air,
He will not lack communion there.
O little think you what he sees
In rivers, brooks, and forest trees;
An elfin band is ever near,
To pipe rich music in his ear.
Here Innocence, with stainless brow,
Reposes 'neath a fragrant bough;
There, Joy, with rapture in his eye,
And dimpled Love, trip blushing by.
And thus he wanders, day by day,
A dreamer on the dusty way;
And morn, and noon, and eventide,
Find some fresh angel at his side.

## THE GHOST OF THE DANE.

TWELVE tolled the bell in the old grey tower,
The prayer was o'er for the dead,
The lights were out in the Abbey hall,
And the Abbot lay in his bed.

The north wind blew on the broken coast,
The waves leaped under the sky.
"God keep the ship from the wild lee shore!"
Was many a landsman's cry.

Out from the dark came the broad full moon,
With the glare of a phantom-light;
Into the dark she shot full soon,
Making a dreary night.

Came down the hill from Abbots-ham,
Each walking timorously,
Three travellers at that gloomy hour,
But not in company.

About a league from Abbots-ham,
A half-league from the sea,
Two furlongs' space from the Northern-ham,
As near as it may be,

A path there was across the down—
A beaten Saxon road—
Hard by, a stone rude-shapen was,
Of monstrous weight, and broad.

Out from the night came the broad full moon,
Out from the dark came she;
While a spectral form, without a shroud,
Spake out imploringly:

"Ho, ho! ho, ho! who goeth there?
Help to relay this stone!
They have roused me from my slumbers here,"
Spake he of the grisly bone.

"Whence comest thou, my good yeoman,
And whither in haste away?"
"From my low-thatched cot near the Abbots-ham,
To the village beside the bay."

Spake the gaunt spectre of grisly bone,
 "Come tarry awhile, I pray."
But the yeoman fled, with his bristling hair,
 To the village beside the bay.

"Ho, ho! ho, ho! my sailor bold,
 Help me this stone to lay."
"I cannot tarry, the night is cold,
 And my ship is under way."

Spake the grim spectre of grisly bone,
 "The yeoman went his way,
And thou shalt lack courage in days to come,
 When thy ship is out of the bay.

"No grace to thy soul when thou comest to die."
 "What?" to the Ghost, quoth he.
"No grace to thy soul when thou comest to die;
 For thou showest no pity to me."

"Ho, ho, there! thou in the huge grey hood,
 Whence dost thou come this way?"
"My goodman lives in the Northern-ham;
 Speak on, what hast to say?"

Spake the gaunt spectre of grisly bone,
Under the dark night sky,
"Some vassal hand hath shifted this stone,
Which over my bones did lie.

"Take courage, for all of womankind
Shall pass in comfort here;
But the yeoman stout and sailor bold
Shall shake for very fear."

"I pledge thee my troth, when the cock hath crowed
And called thee down to rest,
I will pray for the peace of thy troubled soul,
And replace the stone on thy breast."

"God rest thee, good woman, stay awhile,
And trust me faithfully;
And I will tell thee how I came
A ghostly form to be.

"In olden days, the gallant Danes
Came sailing o'er the sea;
And many a battle sore they fought,
In this thy fair country.

"O brave, right brave were the Northern men,
And wild as wolf on the wold;
And brave, right brave was the stout Saxon,
And his king was wise and bold.

"Far, far away in Selwood's shade,
Did valiant Alfred hide;
Who lived on the faith of a better time,
When we sailed o'er the tide.

"O, wild was the sea on that wild day,
When we our troops did land
At Appledore port, inside the bay;
And Hubba held command.

"Hard was the fight we waged with the foe,
As we stood in the blood-stained wave;
But the Saxon band in the strife gave way,
When spake our Hubba brave,

"'There is a chief in Kenwith Hall,
Brave Odun is his name,
The valiant Earl of Devonshire,
Of good and worthy fame.

"'Up yonder is the beaten road,
On to the castle now;
Odun before bold Hubba's sword
His haughty head shall bow.'

"'Comes up a host from the town by the sea,'
Spake the warder upon the wall;
And the blast he blew from his trusty horn
Was heard in Kenwith Hall.

"The Earl was there, with his merry men,
All ready, stout and true.
Let the brown ale rest in its flagon now,
There is ruder work to do.

"The Danes were below the castle wall,
When Hubba spake to his band,
'This tower so strong, my true men all,
No Northman shall withstand.'

"Spake Odun, the Earl of Devonshire,
'Thy Northmen may be true;
But before brave Odun yields his sword,
They have much rough work to do.'

"Swift shot a shower of deadly darts
From their stubborn bows of yew;
And as fast and faster they pierced their hearts,
Faster the arrows flew.

"Many a day, and many a night,
The Northmen dared to stay;
Till the moat with the fierce Danes' blood was red,
As red as the dying day.

"'Now for the charge, my Saxons true!'
And O, 'twas a savage fray;
But the Northmen by the Saxon band
Were driven into the bay.

"On 'Bloody Corner's' trampled sward
I fell among the slain,
As onward rolled the battle wave,
And swept away the Dane.

"And yonder grave by the winding shore,
With seaweed overgrown,
On the eastward side of Appledore,
Is our great Hubba's stone."

Over the clouds sailed the broad full moon,
Like a ship on a troubled sea;
"I am summoned down to the shades below,"
Spake the Ghost, and vanished he.

## JANUS AND HIS DAUGHTERS.

YOUNG JANUS was a comely lad,
A bold and amorous wight,
Who to DECEMBER wedded was
Upon a frosty night.

With laurel crown his brow was bound,
Green ivy made his vest,
And crimson holly-berries shone
In clusters on his breast.

DECEMBER wore a robe of snow,
A necklace made of stars;
The young moon held the bridal torch,
As bright as ruddy Mars.

Old Father Christmas made the feast;
Mirth rang the marriage bell;
The priest was Winter; and the guests
Drank deep of hydromel.

In truth it was a jovial time,
In cottage and in hall;
But I will sing their children born
'Tween spring and winterfall.

The first, pale February, came,
A virgin dressed in white;
A snow-drop, by the maiden worn,
Appeared her chief delight.

The next was March, a lusty lass,
With violet-coloured eye;
She wore a primrose mantelet,
With fringe of orange-dye.

I missed her on a stormy day,
And her sweet sister came,
Girt round about with buttercups,
A coy, capricious dame.

A tear I saw in April's eye,
A blue-bell on her breast;
And soon a lonely cuckoo came
And sang her to her rest.

Then daisy-kirtled MAY I met,
With hawthorn on her head;
And, with a lover's warmest love,
I wooed the bonny maid.

I praised the beauty of her cheek,
Fresh as an April shower:
She blushed like apple-bloom, and said,
"Come hither to my bower."

I followed, and she bade me hear
A minstrel singing high;
"It is for me," she said, "he sings,
Sweet poet of the sky."

Her voice was like the mellow horn
Of blackbird in the spring;
And as I stood admiring her,
Fair JUNE began to sing.

"Lo! here I come with happy days,
The gayest of the year;
See, nature crowneth me with life,
And joy is ever near.

"Behold my rose-buds opening
    By thousands every morn;
See how my poppy-blossoms wave,
    Like banners o'er the corn.

"And I have honeysuckle flowers,
    And summer's princely son,
The foxglove, and poor ragged-Rob,
    With his red jacket on.

"And though no pensive violet
    Is drowsy with the dew,
I've speedwell and forget-me-not,
    And vervain drest in blue.

"Nor care I though the gorse and broom
    Have shaken off their gold,
While hawkweeds and the healing wort
    Of John the saint I hold."

She took me where the bramble-rose
    And azure flax-star grew,
Cow-wheat, and prim-pink-centaury,
    And guelder roses blew.

Where mallow, elder, eyebright, thrift,
And storkbills lined the way;
And wood and water-betony
And ragwort whispered "Stay!"

We sat down on a thymy bank,
And culled sweet cammock flowers,
And bladder wort, and loosestrife plucked,
And talked of bygone hours.

"You know," said she, "when first we met,
I was a ruddy lass,
Sweet with the scent of clover-globes,
And purple-blooming grass——"

Just then a sturdy meader came,
With scythe and cider-horn,
And June, with her red cherry cheeks,
Of all her charms was shorn.

She pined, poor thing! until she died,
Of broken heart, one day;
And a sweet grave they made for her
Of her own fragrant hay.

And now, behold, came dancing in
  Another bonny maid,
With willow-herb and lady-fern,
  And sunshine on her head.

A dress of white convolvulus,
  Inwove with new-shot corn,
With many a graceful grass and leaf,
  By fair JULY was worn.

When, lo! a merry laugh I heard,
  And brown-faced AUGUST came,
Panting beneath a load of fruit,
  A jolly-hearted dame.

A firkin filled with barley-wine
  She carried in her hand,
With rich, ripe clusters from the vine,
  And sweet cake for her band.

I watched her as she sought the fields,
  Where bent the golden ears,
And soon a group of reaping men
  Sent forth their lusty cheers.

One praised her for her golden locks,
One for her harvest team,
Some for her sweet metheglin draught,
Some for her clouted cream.

And many a song was sung for her,
And many a feast she made;
But soon, like her own sheaf-bound flowers,
Her charms began to fade.

Next came, with scarlet pimpernel,
And purple scabious crowned,
September, like a cottage girl,
Red-kerchiefed and blue-gowned.

And when, amidst the golden ferns,
I missed the gentle maid,
October came, with tawny face,
And rainbow-coloured head.

She was a beauty, richly drest,
And wore a courtly train,
Which rustled in the yellow wood,
And trailed along the plain.

A welcome ever greeted her,
    In every village street;
Her orchards gave the poor the fruit
    Which made their presses sweet.

I mourned her loss, for with her went
    The leaves from every spray,
And not a bird but sadder seemed,
    Upon her funeral day.

NOVEMBER was the youngest born,
    A damsel tall and spare,
Who wandering lovelorn in the woods,
    Breathed all her sorrow there.

And when the maiden in her grave
    Was buried cold and low,
Heaven wove for her neglected mound
    A coverlet of snow.

## GOD IN NATURE.

There is a soul doth underlie
The flower we pass unheeded by;
The fire-drops on the plains of night
Show more divinity than light;
And not a blade of grass we see
But hath its hidden mystery.

The silken web the spider weaves
Amid the spring and autumn leaves,
Some busy spirit of the meads
Will string with tiny silver beads;
And there's a hand we cannot see,
That strips each richly laden tree.

Go, mark the cloud that sails on high,
Like phantom ship across the sky,
The bow of beauty stand and view—
Who painted each ethereal hue?—
And list the winds, those wild weird things—
Who plays upon their unseen strings?

Go, stand upon the rocky shore,
And hear the sad and ceaseless roar
Which cometh ever from the main,
As one upon a couch of pain;
Or where the river leaps along,
A silver glory, and a song.

Who gives the colour to the flower;
The star its fire; the sun its power;
Their brightness to the cloud and bow;
And music to the river's flow?
Give answer, thunder—Is it chance
That makes thy solemn utterance?

O Thou, whom winds and waves obey,
Where hast Thou made thy chariot-way?
Oh, whisper from thy throne divine,
And answer me, Thou God benign;
Or teach thy servant, Lord, to see
The universe is full of Thee.

## THE FIRST OF MAY.

THE little lads are playing,
With their rosy sisters straying,
They are out to greet the May-sun,
As he overlooks the hill ;
In the fragrant lanes and meadows,
In the new buds' tiny shadows,
They are telling out their pleasure
With the music of a rill.

The birds their lays are trilling,
The soul with rapture filling ;
And I think upon that season,
When, a merry-hearted boy,
Nimble-footed, with my father,
I wandered forth to gather
The elm-branch and oak-apple,
With a bosom full of joy.

The white clouds, like the blossom
On the black sloe's thorny bosom,
Are floating in the ether,
Athwart the sapphire sky;
And the birds play in the sedges
Of the newly painted hedges;
But a shade is o'er my spirit,
A tear is in my eye.

Aye, my heart is out of keeping
With every thing but weeping,
For the idol which I worshipped
Is sleeping in the tomb.
When the welkin rang with praises,
And the earth was white with daisies,
On the first and fair May-morning
The Angels took her home.

Friends have followed one another—
Mother, Father, Sister, Brother—
To that land without a vision,
Where the weary are at rest:
But, as comes the time for Maying,
One happy spirit straying,

Leaves the pleasant paths of heaven,
To be my Angel-guest.

So the morn I spend in sighing
O'er a grief too deep for crying;
Through the noon I gather flowers
Which she loved while here on earth,
Till I dream I see each feature
Of the ever blessèd creature,
And the morn which broke in sadness
To a pleasure giveth birth.

## THE NEW YEAR.

Hark, how the bells in old St. Mary's Tower
Ring out their welcome to the happy hour;
That time, when Janus, with his double face,
Views past and present from his standing-place.
The ebb-tide yields, to serve the flowing sea;
Both seed and bloom are on the hazel tree;
The Spring is but the child of winter-tide;
The babe will gambol by the coffin's side;
The new moon from the old moon lights her horn;
The new year from the olden year is born;
And the same peal that bade the old year go,
Welcomes the new year with its cap of snow.

## LENA.

Sing no more the praise of wine,
Name it not, the drink divine!
Bacchus ne'er a God had been,
Had the Greeks her beauty seen:
Such intoxication lies
In the witchery of her eyes.

Cupid, silly God of Love,
Must have blinded been by Jove,
Or he ne'er had seen such grace
In the lines of Venus' face;
She, herself, had blushed to see
Such imperial majesty.

Sweet the dew the May-bee sips
From the lilac's purple lips;
Luscious are the globes which shine
On the nectar-yielding vine;
Sweeter, richer is the bliss
Wakened by fair Lena's kiss.

If I am her slave to be,
Welcome, sweet captivity;
I would ask no place of rest
Softer than her snow-white breast.
If her eye an ocean were,
I could bathe for ever there.

O, to see her on the green,
Nature's own adopted queen;
Like the valley-lily, now,
With her polished marble brow,
Asking loud as looks can speak,
"Who can show so fair a cheek?

"Can the eddy in the stream
Brighter than my dimples gleam?
Can the rose upon the tree
Show a bud as fresh as me?
Or the bird within the grove
Sing a truer note of love?"

Hark! All nature answers, "No;
Maid, thy charms all else outdo.

Fairest thou of Flora's train,
Sweetest bird of all the plain;
What the drop is to the sea,
Lena, Beauty is to thee."

## THE LINNET CHOIR.

A LINNET choir sang in a chesnut crown;
A hundred, perhaps, or more;
Till the stream of their song ran warbling down,
And entered a cottage door.
And this was the burden of their lay,
As they piped in the yellow tree,—
"I love my sweet little lady bird,
And I know that she loves me;
Chip, chip, cherry chip, cherry, cherry, cherry chip;
We linnets are a merry band,
A happy company."

It chanced a poet passed that way,
With a quick and merry thought,
And, listening to the roundelay,
His ear their language caught.

Quoth he, as he heard the minstrels sing,
"What heavenly harmony!
I shall steal that song, and carry it home
To my dear family.
Chip, chip, cherry chip, cherry, cherry, cherry chip."
And that song they sing now every eve,
His children, wife, and he.

Next came a boy, with a curly head,
And laughter-lighted eye,
"I've a cage at home, sweet birds," he said,
"And I'll catch you by-and-by;
My sister would feed and love you well,
My mother would happier be;
Come, tell me," he said, "my little birds,
Shall I take you home with me?"
Chip, chip, cherry chip, cherry, cherry, cherry chip;
And all that night the little boy dreamt
He heard the birds in the tree.

Then followed a widow in sable weeds,
Who lightly pressed the land;
She was going to scatter some mignionette seeds
In the graveyard close at hand;

And the birds called up some hidden joys,
  Which lay in her faithful breast;
For she thought how the birds were loved by one,
  Who was now in his quiet rest.
Chip, chip, cherry chip, cherry, cherry, cherry chip.
And the widow will never forget their song,
  Till her sun goes down in the west.

## A PASTORAL ODE,

ON THE DEPARTURE OF THEIR ROYAL HIGHNESSES THE PRINCE AND PRINCESS FREDERICK WILLIAM OF PRUSSIA.

LET others strike the tuneful lyre,
And waken it to mirth;
We'll shed our tears on Hymen's fire,
Beside our cottage hearth.

There was a lamb we called our own,
The favourite of the flock,
Fed by the hand that holds the throne,
Of a right-royal stock.

We hailed its birth for England's sake,
And nursed it day by day;
We watched it, as by brook or lake
Our milk-white pet would play.

Whene'er the sky was overcast
With tempest-boding gloom,
We hid it from the stormy blast,
And turned aside its doom.

And year by year it throve and grew
A soul-inspiring joy,
When sudden o'er its pathway flew
The cruel wingéd boy.

He drew his bow with steady hand,
And, lo! the mystic dart
Struck hard the glory of our land,
And pierced it to the heart.

Now every shepherd's pipe is mute,
Each shepherdess complains,—
But hark! we hear the merry lute,
There's joy among the swains;

Behold! it comes with head erect,
Led by the boy divine,
A captive with a garland decked
Of orange, rose, and vine.

Again, there was a lovely flower,
  The fairest of the fair;
'Twas reared within a royal bower,
  Cherished with pious care:

We saw it bloom beside the throne,
  A bud of promise bright,
In beauty of the softest tone,
  An emblem of delight.

One morn a princely swain passed by
  Our little sea-bound "Close,"
And stole it,—still God speed, we cry,
  Our *England's island-rose*.

Blow softly on the queen of flowers,
  Ye winds that kiss the Rhine;
And long preserve, ye heavenly powers,
  The *rose* to grace the *vine*.

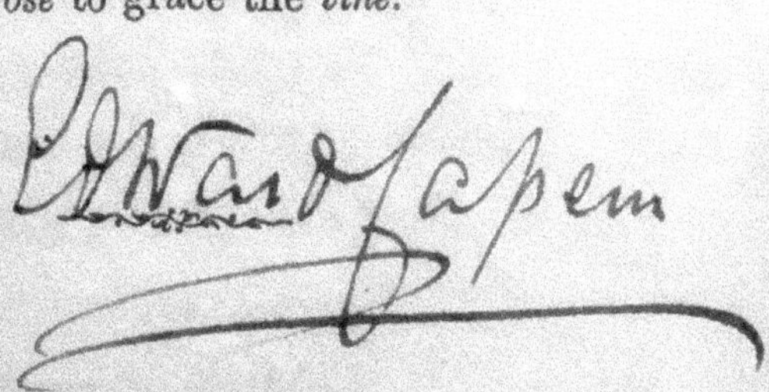

## THE VALES OF DEVONIA.

The vales of Devonia!
What landscapes are seen,
So fertile in beauty,
So golden and green!
There crowfoot and clover
Allure the wild bee,
To gather sweet honey,
For Janie and me.

Thy hills, O Devonia,
Thy meadows and streams,
They haunt me for ever,
In visions and dreams;
The birds in thy woodlands,
Their music is rare;
Thy kine are most famous,
And balmy thy air.

My dear old Devonia,
  What daughters are thine!
As fresh as the morning,
  As sweet as the vine.
The joy of each dwelling,
  In castle or cot;
There's little like heaven
  Where woman is not.

Thy sons, O Devonia!
  Have honoured thy name;
Their deeds are thy poems,
  Their glory thy fame;
And spite of the shadows
  That darkened the sky,
The sun of thy triumph
  Is shining on high.

O, queen of bright rivers,
  In beautiful May,
On fancy's swift pinions
  I hasten away,

To muse where thy waters
  Roll down to the sea,
Fair Exe of Devonia,
  And wander with thee.

Sweet vales of Devonia,
  There's one thing I crave;
Ye gave me a birthplace,
  O give me a grave!
Let it be where the sunshine
  Can warm my last home,
And a knot of your daisies
  Blow over my tomb.

## THE OLD STONE-BREAKER.

Christ befriend thee, poor old man,
With misty eye, and fleshless bone,
Dripping and shivering there alone,
Wrapped in a rag on that cold, cold stone;
Feeble and toothless, haggard and wan,
My heart aches for thee, poor old man.

A stranded wreck by life's rough sea,
The old man raised his eyes and said,
"'Tis a sin to wish that one were dead;
But days together I want for bread;
And Sir, oh Sir, the wretch you see,
Ne'er dreamt he should so aged be."

"Yonder 's the parish house," said I,
"And one so poor and very old
Should seek its refuge from the cold."
"No jail for me, were it built of gold,—

I ever loved the fields and sky;
I would rather sit by this hedge and die.

" When I was young, my sturdy prime
I sold for very nought a week—
A shilling-a-day—the truth I speak,
And my wife and little ones oft were sick;
And now, with my head all white with rime,
You see a victim of ill-paid time.

" 'Tis hard to starve; I sought 'the board;'
They chided me much for being poor;
My memory called up days of yore,
When I made the wood ring and threshing-floor;
And I thought of many a golden hoard,
These shrivelled hands for them had stored.

" My spirit was broken; I turned to go,
When a rough voice thundered, 'Pauper, stay!'
And spoke of an order for three-pence a day:
I have sixpence each week for lodgings to pay;
That is two-pence per day for the six, Sir, you know,
And the seventh I feast on the thoughts of my woe."

"What is thy pittance, poor old man?
  The price of those blows on that stubborn stone,
  That crack, crack, crack, and constant groan?"
  "Two-pence a day," quoth he, with a moan.
Down o'er my cheeks the big tear ran,
And I pitied the fate of that poor old man.

Ye who are wealthy, a lesson learn,—
  Hear what the blessed Jesus said,
  "Give us each day our daily bread;"
  And drive out want from the poor man's shed:
Work him, but love him, and pay him in turn,
And the aged for hunger shall cease to mourn.

Would you have England without a brand?
  Would you have Devon the merry shire?
  See that each poor old withered sire,
  Doomed on its bosom soon to expire,
Dies not an outcast, hammer in hand,
While there's corn in your garner, and gold in the
    land.

## THE FIRST GRIEF.

FAIR Artha came dancing one day to the door,
As light as a fawn on its heath-covered floor;
And bright as a sunbeam with gladness she shone,
For sorrow's dark shadow she never had known.

But one at the threshold stood mournfully there,
With a cloud on her brow like a shade of despair;
"'Twas only but yesterday, Artha," she said,
"Thy linnet was singing, and now it is dead."

And the eye that was lighted grew dark with a
gloom,
That blackness of grief which encircles the tomb.—
O, a wonderful thing is a mirth-lighted eye;
For touch but a spring, and the smile is a sigh.

## THE DINNER-BELL.

The dinner-bell, the dinner-bell,
That dingle dongles through the dell;
I'd rather hear its iron tongue,
Than proudest note of battle-song:
And, 'spite of harp and classic shell,
No music's like the dinner-bell.

The dinner-bell, the dinner-bell,
As out its brazen welcomes swell,
The ploughman slips his weary team,
Indulging in a pleasant dream,
When he shall wed his rosy Nell,
The maid who rings the dinner-bell.

The dinner-bell, the dinner-bell,
There 's not a feud I would not quell,
Throughout the round of England's coast,
If I had Devon beeves to roast;
I'd scatter every mob pell-mell,
And charm them with my dinner-bell.

The dinner-bell, the dinner-bell,
Ah, there 's a sadder tale to tell;
As here and there it plenty rings,
Oh, there are scores of famished things,
Who sniff the dinner's fragrant smell,
And sighing hear the dinner-bell.

The dinner-bell, the dinner-bell,
I love its merry music well;
And if I had a noble's store,
I'd keep a butler for the poor;
And he should ring the laughing knell
Of hunger on my dinner-bell.

## SOLACE.

Weep not, for the good bequeath us
  Much that is immortal still;
Like the meek example Jesus
  Left us in His life and will.

Love 's a portion of the spirit
  Far too subtile for the tomb;
And if each that joy inherit,
  Every heart 's an angel's home.

Tell me, good and gentle brother,
  Frankly be the truth confessed,
You who mourn a sainted mother,
  Is she now an absent guest?

And the flower you dreamt had perished,
  Doth it not more living seem?
Say, the babe you fondly cherished,
  Smiles it not in every dream?

Death 's a dark and frozen river
  To the mourner's weeping eyes ;
But an under-current ever
  Runs, of thought that never dies.

Weep not, then, for this is certain :
  When our precious ones depart,
Love, that lifts Death's sable curtain,
  Finds them pictured on the heart.

# SYMPATHY.

In passing through this lovely world,
  I little heed a trial;
And ever strive to keep unfurled
  The flag of self-denial.
I mourn sometimes, with sorrow deep,
  For friends, like any other;
But a large stock of smiles I keep
  For comforting a brother.

Oh, 'tis a blessed thing to live
  In sympathy with sorrow;
And help the mourner to believe
  That joy will come to-morrow.
Let selfish mortals seek repose,
  With an unruffled feather;
My neighbour's wrongs shall be my woes,
  And we will feel together.

## MARRIAGE SONG.

Joy, joy, joy,
  Wherefore should we sorrow?
Care, old Care—
  Let him come to-morrow!
Love weds love,
  Nought on earth is fitter;
Why, then, why
  Tears to make it bitter?

Hark, hark, hark,
  How the bells are ringing.
Come, come, come,
  Let us all be singing.
Joy, joy, joy,
  Music, mirth, and laughter,
Now, now, now,
  And to all hereafter.

## THE VIOLET.

WHERE Torridge laves its banks of green,
A rustic cottage may be seen,
Drooping its unaspiring head,
Like some retiring rustic maid
Who shuns her lover's bold advance,
Yet steals beneath her hat a glance.
A little, unpretending cot,
Which fell to blest contentment's lot;
A shrine of art; a home of loves,
In a sweet miniature of groves.
With reed its roof is neatly thatched,
Where various callow broods are hatched.
Beneath the clipt and moss-crowned eaves,
And sheltered much by ivy leaves,
A shady roof—supported o'er
By pillars rising from the floor,
Round which rich honeysuckles twine,
Domestic rose, and jessamine—
Repels the too intruding sun,
And gives the scene a cooler tone.

'Twas on a calm and sunny day
In March that I betook my way
Unto its green and peaceful shade,
In Fancy's person to invade.
I entered at the rustic gate,
And stole to where the family sate
Within a little gothic hall.
I glanced around, and lo! each wall
Was hung with paintings everywhere;
But one among the rest, more fair
Than any that my eyes could see,
Induced a silent reverie.
Above the mantel-shelf it hung,
Nor did I need a friendly tongue
To tell me that the forms I saw
Were painted from the group below.
Around the breakfast table, there
Were seated, each in antique chair,
The members of the family,
The matron, sire, and children three;
And, seeing one sweet pictured face
Was missing from her wonted place,
I wondered much, as there I stood,
And watched the scene which then ensued.

The breakfast over, and a prayer
To Him who blessed them with His care,
The mother to the father brought
A present, and his blessing sought.
Close following, a lively maid
Tripped lightly up, and smiling said,
"A posy from your daughter take,
And keep it for her own dear sake."
And then there came a lovely boy,
With eye-balls swelling out with joy,
And, climbing up his parent's knee,
"Some birthday violets, too," said he.
I marked the loving parents' eyes,
And thought I heard some heavy sighs,
As oft as with their sight they met
Each sweetly-scented violet.
Another moment passed away,
When I beheld their glances stray
Towards the painting on the wall,
And then a sobbing filled the hall,
For pent-up grief broke forth at last.
Twelve tearful months had nearly passed
And yet the maiden in the tomb
Was still the blossom of their home.

"Where are her violets, dearest pet?"
The mother sobbed, "sweet violet."
And soon a precious stream of tears
Ran down the cheeks of younger years,
Till e'en the sturdy sire was seen
A weeper in that lovely scene;
And all I heard was fond regret,
Re-echoing "sweet violet."

## 'TIS PRIMROSE TIME AGAIN.

The sun is smiling on the day;
  And, high upon the wing,
The lark pours forth his sweetest lay
  Into the ear of Spring.
The lusty thrush, in merry mood,
  Pipes out his loudest strain;
And children shout, from wood to wood,
  "'Tis primrose time again."

The willow buds are swathed in down;
  The hazel is in bloom;
The hawthorn wears a richer brown;
  And greener grows the broom.
Hark, every bird, in bush and tree,
  Cries, "Must we sing in vain?
Come out, ye brick-bound souls, be free—
  'Tis primrose time again."

"Come, wife, my love, away—away
  To mossy cave and bower;
Or let us in our shadows play
  With Nature one short hour.
Thou and the wee folk now are well,
  To-morrow it may rain;
My heart is ringing like a bell,
  'Tis primrose time again."

## THE FORESIGN.

"I fear that Jemmy's ship is lost,"
  Said old Joanna May;
"I dreamt the 'Wellington' went down
  In Biscay's stormy bay.
Three times I dreamt—and Peter too—
  That Jem was cast away.

"Poor boy, he was a precious child,
  A jewel unto me;
Although, like every water-bird,
  He was a bit too free.
I'm sure I shall be driven wild
  If he is lost at sea."

"Tell me your dream."—"I dreamt I stood
  Upon a wild, wild shore,
And Jem was washed in at my feet;
  I dreamt it o'er and o'er.
He saw 'twas I, and tried to speak,
  I woke, and saw no more.

"And then beside a frowning rock,
Exhausted on the crags,
I thought I saw his bleeding form,
Half clad in dripping rags;
And all this time the waves ran high,
And leaped like hunted stags.

"Again—I heard him at my door;
He called us by our names.
I woke up—'Peter, there,' said I,
'That surely was our James!'
It was a dream—I slept again,
And saw the ship in flames.

"To-day, I heard the ship went down,
And every hand, almost,
Was drowned, or cast on shore to die
Upon a barren coast.
Ah, Sir, I know my dream is true—
Last night I saw his ghost."

## THE SAILOR'S BRIDE.

SHE is sitting in her cottage,
  Amid the flowers of May;
The birds are singing merrily,
  The children are at play;
But her heart weeps in its widowhood,
  For William is away.

Her pretty cot is furnished
  With many sea-shells rare;
A snow-white board, a faithful clock,
  And ancient double chair;
But comforts make it comfortless,
  Since William is not there.

Three long years were they parted—
  Young Mary Ann and he.
He was the boldest sailor lad,
  The truest maid was she;
And Love had made the twain but one,
  So well did they agree.

Fast flew the happy moments
  That hastened on the day
When joy, in full fruition,
  Their patience should repay;
A letter Mary Ann received,
  Said he was on his way.

A ship is off the Foreland,
  She sees it from her door;
One hour, and then her William
  Is safe upon the shore.
Another week—they wedded are,
  She dreams, to part no more.

She is sitting in her cottage,
  No William smiling near;
A drop is on her marble hand,
  She muses on the tear,
And seems as if she listened
  To some one at her ear.

Three moons ago, the happiest
  Of womankind was she;
Young William bold was at her side,

A merry fellow he.
Now, she is lonely in her home;
He, lonely on the sea.

Her cheeks, which made the red rose pale,
Are now as white as snow;
His heart, unconquered in the war,
Is beating soft and slow.
He writes, "I'm sick at heart, dear wife;"
She writes, "I'm full of woe."

They little dreamt, when walking,
The merriest of earth,
That sorrow was to laughing joy
So near allied in birth.
He pineth for the love of her;
She flies the sound of mirth.

And, weeping in her cottage,
Amid the flowers of May,
She heedeth not the singing birds,
Or little ones at play;
And says, 'tis worse than widowhood
To have her love away.

Go to the village churchyard—
  A new-made grave is there.
Go, ask the man outside her cot
  Whose letter he doth bear?
Another moon, the widower
  With grief will wet his hair.

## THE BEREAVED ONE.

Did you know my little blue-eyed maid?
As light as a fawn's was her velvet tread.
O, how she'd laugh and loudly sing;
With her it was ever one bright Spring.

She used to sing—in her own sweet way—
That angels came on each first Spring day,
And wiled away their pleasant hours,
In strewing earth with lovely flowers.

I have heard her shout, in her midnight dreams,
"There, there they come on the bright sunbeams!"
And next morn she would wander to and fro,
To track their footprints in the snow.

Twelve months ago, this very day,
Like a child going out in the sun to play,
She died; but ere she closed her eyes,
She filled my soul with a sad surprise.

"Mother," said she, "I am going home,
By the path I saw the angels come;
And every year, if that may be,
I'll come and strew Spring flowers for thee."

Smile not, but once a year I go,
To gather these violets winged with snow;
And then I always think I hear
My precious angel warbling near.

## THE LITTLE SCARE-CROW.

She is up in yonder field,
  Mid the new-sown corn;
She'll be there until the eve,
  She has been there since the morn.
O, the pretty little creature,
  With her bright blue eye,
I heard her noisy clapper,
  And her scare-crow cry.

I paused to mark the child—
  She was very pale and young;
She told me "she was six,"
  With her merry little tongue.
In her hand she held her hat,
  Which the wild wind swayed;
And purple were the feet
  Of the scare-crow maid.

More happy than a queen,
  Though scanty was her food,
The child that sang her song
  To that clapper-music rude.
This the maiden's simple lay,
  As she warbled in her nook,
" Here, clapping every day,
  I scare the robber-rook ! "

## THE BRIDAL.

The banner waves o'er Tapley Hall;
The minstrels wait to play;
Young Caroline the beautiful
Weds with her lord to-day.

The marriage guests in clusters group,
The bridegroom he is there,
With noble Portsmouth, Chichester,
And many a lady fair.

Young men and maidens shout their joy
In park and village lane;
And e'en a sign of gladness flaunts
O'er Westleigh's solemn fane.

The bride is in her chamber lone,
A May-day rose, in tears;
Assured that hope and happiness
Will bless her future years,

Why grieves the pride of Tapley Hall,
The flower of Clevland's race?
'Tis for her widowed mother there,
The angel of the place.

Spake the fond mourner,—"Shall my woe
Mix with thy cup of life,
When Love is waiting with his crown
To make the maiden wife?

"Go, bind the orange round thy brow,
Call in thy faithful maid;
'Tis when the cruel storm is high
The daisy droops its head."

As the proud sun dispels the mists,
She scattered all her fears,
And the rose blossomed on her cheek,
More lovely for her tears.

So have I seen an ebon cloud,
Near the moon's silver face,
Grow brighter as it nearer drew,—
A beauty and a grace.

But who is she, with fawn-like step,
Majestic as the morn;
With voice so soft and silverly
As 'twere Apollo's horn?

It is her wedded sister; she,
In jewelled kirtle drest,
Proclaims the marriage hour is come,
To all the lady-guests.

Like unto clouds of gossamer,
With fairy forms of light,
And wreathed with sapphire are her maids,
All clad in virgin white.

Down-vestured, like a flock of swans,
To their hymeneal cars
They glide, while Caroline walks forth,
A moon among the stars.

Within the temple, laurel crowned,
What language e'er can speak
The charms that dance within her eyes,
And chase across her cheek.

As Parian marble, lily pure,
  Or snowdrop in the lane,
She seems amid the rainbow lights
  That glimmer through the pane.

Oh, with what reverence she kneels
  Beside that altar there,—
Whilst joy, hard throbbing in her soul,
  Is tempered down to prayer.

As one of Raphael's pictured saints,
  The bridegroom by her side
Waits with the pledge of married love
  To ring the peerless bride.

'Tis o'er! the sacred rite is o'er!
  The merry tell-tales ring;
"They're married, and God bless the match,"
  The honest peasants sing.

The horses paw the gravel paths
  Which thread the spacious lawn;
The chariot is before the gate,
  They enter—and are gone.

Fling high the slipper in the air!
The lucky trifle throw;—
A simple custom, but may reach
Where words can scarcely go.

Now let your mirth sound through the hall,
With loud outringing tone;—
But know, the widowed mother sits
And, childless, prays alone.

## POLLY LEE.

"Polly Lee, Polly Lee,
What's your hurry, Polly Lee?
Don't you know, in company
Journeys shorten pleasantly?"

"Jesse Gay, Jesse Gay,
You have heard my mother say,
Men are troubles in our way,
Jesse Gay, Jesse Gay."

"Polly Lee, Polly Lee,
Listen, honey—don't you see
That was never meant for me,
Polly Lee, Polly Lee?"

"Jesse Gay, Jesse Gay,
You are joking, Jesse, eh?
Fie! for all the maidens say
You're in love with Fanny May."

"Nay, my pretty Polly Lee,
That can never, never be;
Like that bird upon the tree
One I love—and that is thee!"

Jesse Gay, Jesse Gay
Made her rosy blushes play,
Blind she grew, and missed her way,
All for love of Jesse Gay.

Wooed to wed, said Polly Lee,
"Jesse, you must wait a wee."
"Well, a month,—and then," said he,
"Polly Gay thy name shall be."

Another moon—the marriage moon—
Alas for Jesse, came too soon;
May went, and sent in bonny June,
But death came with the bridal noon.

"Jesse Gay, Jesse Gay,
Why so sad, and where away?"
"Yonder rose-strewn grave to see;
My heart lies there with Polly Lee."

## KATE.

WHERE the upland, overhanging,
Looks on "Torridge," far below,
Creeping by its banks of rushes,
Till it mingles with the "Taw,"

There, among the hazel bushes,
And the elms upon its slope,
Violet-like, 'mid ferns and mosses,
Grew this little bud of hope.

Kate, the maiden of the cottage,
Kate, a little forest flower,
Nursed within the green wood's bosom,
Like a rose within a bower.

Fair as snow upon the winter,
Fairer than the lily she,
Or the moon's own silver image,
Pictured on a quiet sea.

Bright as light-tipt clouds that wander
  Noiseless o'er their fields of blue,
Brighter than the flowers of summer,
  Or the rainbow's rosy hue.

Oft I meet her in the morning,
  Tripping o'er the dusty road,
Smiling 'neath a shady bonnet,
  Plaited, brown, and amply broad.

Is it spring? she bears a posy,
  Made of wild flowers to her mood.
Is it summer? then sweet roses
  Blush beside green southern-wood.

In the autumn days, the wheat-ear,
  And the scabious' purple plume,
With the creepers of the corn-field,
  Meet with scarlet poppies' bloom.

And when winter on the yew tree
  Soft vermilion bells hath spread,
Then she plucks the bay and laurel,
  And the holly, green and red.

Sometimes she will fain be friendly,
  Then a smile her wish betrays;
And I halt to learn the secret,
  And to mark her simple ways.

All this time I watch her ringlets,
  Dancing on her healthful cheek,
And the charms that play in dimples
  Round the cherry lips that speak.

Then the parting salutation
  Having passed, I turn away,
Thanking Heaven such lovely creatures
  Meet and bless us day by day.

## PATTY ROWE.

In her cot upon the hill,
Where the rude winds blow,
Sitting by the sill,
Is pretty Patty Rowe.
O, the little merry lass,
Whene'er I see her pass,
Like the dew-drops on the grass
Shine her dark eyes, O.

To see her 'neath the eaves
Of her cottage low,
Peeping through the leaves
Of the green vines, O;
And to hear the maiden sing,
Like a linnet in the spring,
Is to wish one had the ring
Then to wed her, O.

It happened on a day,
  A wild day, O,
A stranger chanced to stay
  In her cottage low;
When the lassie with a smile,
And a sweet bewitching wile,
Sang "Meet me by the stile,"
  To the laddie, O.

He felt the tender flame
  In his bosom glow;
And asking her her name,
  Strove in vain to go.
The moments quickly passed,
For Love had chained him fast;
"I ne'er," said he, at last,
  "Felt so happy, O."

Young Patty fed his fire
  With her love songs, O,
While he, behind her sire,
  Twitched her dark locks so;

At length her pouting lips
He pressed, and sang out "Slips!"
Then they played at apple-pips,
  All for love, or no.

Now round about the house
  The maid doth go,
Nimble as a mouse,
  Enchanted, O.
Day and night she dreams of Phil,
In her cot upon the hill——
Hark! I hear the wedding peal;
  They are married, O!

## DOLLY DANE.

HAST thou ever felt the smart, Dolly Dane,
Of a love-bestricken heart, Dolly Dane?
  Though about with ivory bound,
  Oft that thief will there be found,
Prowling round, and round, and round, Dolly Dane.

'Tis a very subtile thing, Dolly Dane;
Flying oft on airy wing, Dolly Dane;
  Through the portals of the eyes
  Often unobserved it flies,
Or it melts away in sighs, Dolly Dane.

Do not prate of one to give, Dolly Dane,
For it may one day deceive, Dolly Dane.
  Cupid lives by sporting, know,
  And the arrow of his bow,
Strung with hearts, one day I saw, Dolly Dane.

Say, oh say not thine is right, Dolly Dane;
Much deceived was my sight, Dolly Dane,
  If the little rogue divine,
  Did not laugh, and show me thine,
Wedded very close to mine, Dolly Dane.

## THE STRANGER'S GRAVE AT NORTHAM.

'Twas a rude and bitter time, that night;
The storm fiend was abroad,
And many a gallant "homeward bound"
Went down on her ocean road.

Like fury, with a fierce delight
The clouds went sweeping by;
Till the moon put out her silver light,
And the stars fled from the sky.

Next morn, before the sun arose,
I looked towards the bay,
And thought I saw a stranded wreck,
Like a cloud in the misty grey.

I hastened down, in time to see
The little boat go out;
And oh, I never shall forget
How the wild waves leapt about!

And how the winds howled in the shrouds,
  Where the drowning seamen clung;
But the vessel made a fatal lurch,
  And their dirge by the sea was sung.

We buried the drowned, as one by one
  They washed in from the sea;
And we mourned, as even their own would mourn,
  For the dead beneath that tree.

## RUSTIC CHIVALRY.

As Willy his Milly went wooing one day,
Where Ben of the Barton was tossing his hay,
Young Milly to Willy had nothing to say;
So Willy from Milly went sighing away.

Poor Willy ran home in a fury, to write,
And thus to his rival began to indite,—
"As Milly is mine both by promise and right,
Young Ben of the Barton I'm ready to fight."

Ben took up the challenge, and wagers were made,
That Willy would beat burly Ben of the spade:
And Milly, the wicked and rosy-faced jade,
Declared she would have the best man of the trade.

They fought for an hour, by the march of the sun,
And found that hard cuffing was terrible fun;
When Ben of the Barton cried out "I have done,"
And Milly proclaimed that her Willy had won.

## SONG OF THE GIPSY QUEEN.

To roam with the Gipsy King
    Is the happiest life for me;
To dwell where the woodbirds sing,
    And rills dance merrily:
To sit in the sultry shade,
    Through the joyous summer day,
Of a primrose dappled glade,
    Where squirrels leap and play:
To camp in a sunny nook,
    And watch my dark eyes gleam
Like gems in the glassy brook,
    O this is the Gipsy's dream!

Away with your pictured halls,
    And couches soft as down;
Your crimson-coloured walls
    Are scorned by the Gipsy brown:

My roof is the vaulted sky;
    My wall is the sheltering wood;
My mirror my love's bright eye;
    My wine the crystal flood.
My couch is the tufted grass,
    On a bank by the old roadside,
Where the lad, if he chance to pass,
    Will ask for his future bride.
So a tent 'mid the old oak trees,
    For my babe, my love, and me;
Where we'll sit when the winters freeze,
    And only shake with glee.

## RUTH.

You know those little stepping-stones
Where we were wont to meet,
As softly-murmuring waters made
Sweet music at our feet.

There were primrose tufts along the bank,
And gorse-bloom for the bees;
And many a mossy charm was thrown
About the wave-washed trees.

You recollect that morning bright
I whispered in your ear
The virgin words of love's delight,
When hope had nought to fear.

Oh, Ruth, methinks I see you now,
Beside that silver stream;
With love's young blush upon your brow,
The angel of my dream.

Methinks I see your heaving breast,
 Your pretty downcast look,
And feel the warm round cheek I pressed
 Beside that prattling brook.

And, then, the lifting of your lash,
 The glancing of your eye,
Which seemed a violet peeping through
 The leaves to watch the sky.

The love-seal of your coral lips;
 The kiss I thought divine;
All these are pictured on this heart—
 This sad true heart of mine.

And well I know the words I said,
 Just where that dog-rose blew,
"That rose," I breathed, "my gentle maid,
 Is not so fair as you."

Oh, no! it could not be so fair,
 Nor truer could it be;
That rose is withered, you are frail,
 And false as fair to me.

Here—take this treasure! 'twas for you
I ploughed the ocean wild;
To distant lands again I go;
The gold give to your child.

I will not dwell upon the vow
You fondly made to me;
The heart 's the grave of broken loves,
There let mine buried be.

## PITY THE ROSES THAT WITHER WITHIN.

O WHY, my sweet youth, are you plaintively sighing,
O'er roses which, withered, lie scattered around?
Just gaze, and you'll see e'en the flowers, in their dying,
Strew charms o'er those cultureless patches of ground.
"But we," said a voice, "are despised and neglected,
And maidenhood almost is counted a sin;
Come, cease your repining, and woo the rejected;
O pity the roses that wither within.

"We heard you, fair youth, as you stood in the garden,
Find fault with your fate, that your life was so lone;
Now really, we think, but we blushing ask pardon,
That soon you might sing in a merrier tone.

Behold us, a beautiful rosy half-dozen;
  Excuse us, but seeing you will not begin,
If not as a lover, pray call as a cousin,—
  O pity the rosebuds that wither within!"

## DORKY MAY.

HERE'S a lay for Dorky May,
  Let the song go merrily;
One so fair, with charms so rare,
  Blooms but seldom, verily.

O that face and form of grace,
  Made so lithe and slenderly;
Never sprite of love and light
  Smiled so soft and tenderly.

With her cheek the zephyrs seek
  To dally oft admiringly;
And the sun hath often shone
  In her eyes inquiringly.

In a vest of lilac drest,
  Neat, and looking lovingly;
'Tis her sin all hearts to win,
  Then to chide reprovingly.

In the dance, with killing glance,
  Many lovers maketh she;
Joseph, John, and every one,
  As her favourite taketh she.

Near a stile, with artful smile,
  Sweet as April melody,
"I am glad," unto a lad,
  "Thus to meet you," once said she.

Beat his heart, as if 't would part,
  "Do you love me, Dork?" said he.
Quoth she, "Dear, aye, never fear,
  You, and all the lads," said she.

Down the hill, towards the mill,
  Turned the maiden trippingly,
Like a lamb beside its dam,
  Bonny, blithe, and skippingly.

Sing a lay for Dorky May,
  Let the song go merrily;
But beware of Dorky's snare,
  Or she'll kill a score of ye.

## MY BONNY BELL.

My bonny Bell, my bonny Bell,
A sacred story I could tell;
And wert thou in my hawthorn bower,
Some moonlit eve, but one short hour,
That little secret, I know well,
I'd breathe to thee, my bonny Bell.

My bonny Bell, my bonny Bell,
Come, let us down to Fernydell;
The fields are carpeted with gold,
The cuckoo-bird is growing bold;
And I, like him, my love would tell,
My bonny Bell, my bonny Bell.

My bonny Bell, my bonny Bell,
Fairer than fairest asphodel,
Are the milk-white and violet streaks
That ring the roses on thy cheeks;
And sweeter than the hydromel
Thy breathings are, my bonny Bell.

My bonny Bell, my bonny Bell,
What means that sigh? Come, prithee, tell.
Is it the language of thy breast,
And asking to be nearer pressed?
So be it then. One kiss. Farewell,
My bonny Bell, my bonny Bell!

## SAMMY WENT A WOOING.

Sammy went a wooing,
Ding, down, delly,
Whistling and cooing,
Ding, down, delly.
Sammy, he was shy,
Tammy, she was sly,
So they met, and looked awry,
Ding, down, delly.

Down in Orleigh grove,
Ding, down, delly,
Sam was wont to rove,
Ding, down, delly.
Weather wet or fair,
Sammy, he was there;
Tam passed him with an air,
Ding, down, delly.

When Sam was with his wain,
Ding, down, delly,
His heart was sore with pain,
Ding, down, delly.
So Sam resolved to try
The virtue of a cry,
And saying "he should die,"
Ding, down, delly.

'Twas on a summer's day,
Ding, down, delly,
The singing birds were gay,
Ding, down, delly.
Sam told her of his worth,
His pedigree and birth;
Tam kicked the dust with mirth,
Ding, down, delly.

Poor Sammy went away,
Ding, down, delly,
And met with Nelly Gray,
Ding, down, delly.

She saw his heart was sad,
So she gossipped with the lad,
"You're in love," said Nell, "or mad,"
Ding, down, delly.

Now Sammy told her all—
Ding, down, delly—
His troubles, great and small,
Ding, down, delly.
She heard him to the end,
Said, "The matter I can mend,
If you'll listen to a friend,"
Ding, down, delly.

Tam's heart was all on flame,
Ding, down, delly,
She longed to change her name,
Ding, down, delly.
With Cupid—silly thing!—
She played till he took wing,
For Nelly wears the ring—
Bravo, Nelly!

## NANCY DOWNING.

EVER frowning, ever frowning,
  O how dark the world would be,
If, my little Nancy Downing,
  Every maiden frowned like thee.

What's the use of sunshine, Nancy,
  And the warblers of the spring,
If they do not stir our fancy,
  And inspire our lips to sing?

Hark! the primrose lanes are ringing
  With the little children, now;
And the bonny birds are singing,
  Joyous, on the budding bough.

Come, my little Nancy Downing,
  Let me win one smile from thee—
No? Then, if you will be frowning,
  Prithee, do not frown on me.

## THE RIVALS.

Young Peggy and Nancy, so loving were they,
That ever together the maidens would stray;
If one went a milking the other must go,
And none dreamt their love a whit colder would grow.

If Peg bought a bonnet, poor Nancy would try
The very same pattern and colour to buy;
If Nance went to church, there Peg must go too,
And both, dressed in lilac, would sit in one pew.

If Nance had a secret, for Nancy no rest
Till Peggy had got it safe lodged in her breast;
And if Bill, the ploughman, e'er praised Peggy's eyes,
Young Nancy next day on the subject was wise.

Thus things went on pleasant, as pleasant could be,
Till Matty, the miller, came Nancy to see;
He spoke of her locks, and the rose on her cheek,
Her mouth, and blue eyes, as a lover will speak.

Now Nance was in love, if the truth I must tell,
And Peg had a mind to the miller as well;
So Nancy to Peggy the matter conveyed,
And Peggy to Matty her folly betrayed.

The very next revel, young Peggy was seen
With Matty, the miller-boy, footing the green;
Whilst Nancy looked on, like a maid in disgrace,
Who had "cut off her nose just to spite her own face."

It chanced, as young Matty the miller went by,
He saw there was sorrow in Nancy's bright eye;
So, leaving fair Peggy, to Nancy he went,
And Nancy to Matty was married, that Lent.

## THE OLD-FASHIONED PLOUGH.

HERE'S a song for the old-fashioned plough, boys,
The friend of the rich and the poor;
There is nought like the honest old plough, boys,
To keep off grim want from the door.
There 's a spell in the trusty old plough, boys,
There 's a charm in its glossy-backed team,
Which can never be beaten, I vow, boys,
By all the new wonders of steam.

CHORUS.

Then hurrah! for the old-fashioned plough, boys,
And hurrah! for the children of toil;
May God ever speed the good plough, boys,
And prosper the sons of the soil.

The world in its infancy used it,
And its children are proving it now;
Our forefathers never abused it,
And we'll not dishonour the plough.

As wide as the world is its fame, boys,
  Its virtues there 's none can deny;
Like the plough let us win a good name, boys,
  And leave it behind when we die.
          Then hurrah! &c.

When our island with war was distressed, boys,
  And tyranny stood in the prow,
O, who battled for us the best, boys?
  The heroes who followed the plough.
And who, if a foe were to dare, boys,
  To land on our ocean-bound isle,
Would meet them?—the men of the share, boys,
  And take out their pluck for awhile.
          Then hurrah! &c.

But long as the summer-time comes, boys,
  May peace be the lot of us all,
The rose that shall bloom in our homes, boys,
  And cheer both the great and the small;
May our lives be as straight as our furrows,
  And happiness smile on each brow,
Fair wages diminish our sorrows,
  And plenty e'er follow the PLOUGH.
          Then hurrah! &c.

## COTTAGE LOVE.

"Meet me down in Lovers'-lane,
There by the trysting stile,
About a gunshot from the church,
And from your cot a mile.

"I told my poor old mother, love,
I'd take you home to-day;
So, when the bells begin to chime,
Come, Annie dear, away."

A smile of winning tenderness
Curled round the maiden's eye;
She knew that Johnny's love was pure
As aught beneath the sky.

So, to her low-thatched cot she tripped,
As playful as a fawn;
And watched her lover climb the hill
Beside the mansion lawn.

'Twas just two hours after noon,
  When, full of love's delight,
With roses in his button-hole,
  And bells of lily-white,

John hastened down the lass to greet,
  In cottage-lilac dressed,
And met her with a posy sweet
  Upon her bonny breast.

Not half so musical the bells
  Which blessed their ears that day,
As were the love-notes chanted there,
  Along the fragrant way.

And, sooth, it was a goodly sight
  That happy pair to see,
As Johnny pressed fair Annie's lips,
  Beneath the hawthorn tree.

By meadow, hamlet, orchard, stream,
  The winding pathway ran;
By warbling steep, and silent wild,
  Untenanted by man.

And not a flower that bloomed around,
  Or bird upon the tree,
But seemed to give their welcome words,
  And hail their company.

Before a little cottage-door,
  At length the lovers stood,
O'er-arched with rose and jessamine,
  And green with southern-wood.

A honeysuckle, bending down,
  Kissed Annie's blushing cheek,
As through the diamond-lattice panes
  A voice was heard to speak:

"Come in, come in, my children, come,
  Right glad am I to see
Thee, and thy chosen lassie, John—
  Thou canst not make too free.

"Now don't be over-bashful, dear,
  Thou'rt welcome to my shed."
And then the good old woman poured
  A blessing on her head.

A twelvemonth from that very day
  The merry church-bells told
A pair of happy villagers
  Had bought the ring of gold.

A lovely train of laughing maids
  Marched 'neath the linden boughs ;
And John and Annie had fulfilled
  Their holy marriage vows.

## LITTLE COME-BY-CHANCE.

Poor little Come-by-chance
Wept in the rain!
Starving and shivering,
Weary with pain,
Ragged and shoeless,
Pallid and lean,
Poor little Come-by-chance
Stood in the rain.

Poor little Come-by-chance!
Nobody knew
Who were her parents,
They cared little, too.
Wild was the tempest,
Fast fell the snow,
And winter had bitten
Her little feet raw.

By little Come-by-chance
  Swung an old gate;
Inside, a palace
  Where Death sat in state.
A mud-pool, and hovel
  Where swine held the sway;
With old wooden windows
  To bar out the day.

Wild blow the hailstones
  Over the snow;
Hark! there 's a groan
  From a pallet of straw!
Darkness within,
  And a heap on the floor,
Where her poor grandmother
  Dies by the door.

Wealth in its chariot
  Sees nothing wrong;
Waggons, corn-laden,
  Are rumbling along:

Poor little Come-by-chance
  Sits by her home,
The ghost of a little one
  Ripe for the tomb.

Her eye is unclosed,
  Yet dumb is the maid ;
And dropped on her bosom
  Her innocent head !
Her sorrow is over,
  Her suffering and wrong—
Her soul is an angel,
  Her wail is a song.

A hole in the grave-yard
  Is dug the next day ;
And both, without mourners,
  Are buried straightway.
A "shell" is let down—
  Then, a small wooden chest—
And Come-by-chance sleeps
  On her grandmother's breast.

## MY FRIEND IN THE WOOD.

METHOUGHT a thrush upon a tree
Sweetly sang one day to me,
"Poet, poet, hear me, hear me!"
"Hear thee," I at once replied;
"Honest fellow, aye, with pride."
And then he poured out such a tide
Of joy to cheer me.

"Happy, happy bird," said I,
"Ever would I linger by."
"Poet, poet, hear me, hear me!"
Loud and louder yet he sang,
Till the distant woodlands rang
With his wild and merry clang;
And all to cheer me.

So, a minstrel in the shade,
To a brother of the trade
  Oft will warble, "Poet, hear me!
Thou hast felt the witching spell,
Nature works in every dell;
So, from out my hidden cell,
  Let me cheer thee."

## THE SONG OF THE WAITS.

WAKEN, sleeper! from thy dream,
Listen to the heavenly theme:
"Christ is born," the angels hymn,
"Born a babe in Bethlehem."
"Glory be to God on high,"
Is the carol of the sky;
"Peace on earth the infant brings,
Babe of babes, and King of kings."

He the promised seed of old,
He the prophets long foretold,
Shepherds, you may now behold
As a babe in Bethlehem.

Leave your flocks upon the plain,
Haste to swell the wondering train,
He, the Saviour of men,
Sleeps a babe in Bethlehem.

In a manger He is laid,
Mothered by a Jewish maid;
Swaddled in a strawy bed,
    Lies the babe of Bethlehem.

Enter ye within the door,
Kneel upon the sacred floor,
And the holy child adore,
    Christ, the babe of Bethlehem.

Guided by a heavenly star,
Lo, the wise men from afar
Offering their presents are
    To the babe of Bethlehem.

Where the gentle oxen lay,
Feeding on the fragrant hay,
Seer and shepherd hie away
    To the babe of Bethlehem.

God is great and good, we see,
Glorious in humility,
He hath honoured poverty.
    Christ, the babe of Bethlehem.

Waken, sleeper! come, arise!
Join the anthem of the skies;
Christ is come, our sacrifice,
He the babe of Bethlehem.
"Glory be to God on high,"
Chant the carol of the sky;
Peace on earth the infant brings,
Babe of babes, and King of kings.

## MONITIONS.

HAST seen the rainbow of the flowery May
Stretch through the heavens its many-coloured band,
And crown the day;

A dimpled, fair, and bonny blue-eyed maid;
A lily with two violets in a nook,
In smiles arrayed;

An infant nestled in its mother's arms,
Looking into the bright heaven of her eyes,
A group of charms;

A rose, rich as a cherry-parted lip;
A dew-pearl, which the little honey bees
Delight to sip;

The sun walk proudly from his orient gate;
The star of eve attend the queenly moon
In regal state;

The Spring, whose happy duty all day long
Is just to wash her robe of gold and green,
And sing her song;

The Summer, in her hey-day of delight;
Then hast thou lost them, as the stars are lost
Some darksome night?

If so,—Live for THE WORLD WHICH IS TO BE,
Where more than all the beauty thou hast seen
Thine eyes shall see.

## AN AUTUMN INVITATION.

Come out into the woodlands, love,
Before the trees are bare;
The woodlark singeth on the hill
His sweetly mellow air.

A smile is seen on Autumn's cheek,
As one who hath a store;
The bees are in the ivy-bloom,
Above the abbey door.

Come out, before the dark days come,
With blasts and heavy rains:
Come out, before the winter binds
The earth in icy chains.

The air is soft as eider-down;
And brown October's eye
Is looking out to woo thee forth
Beneath its sapphire sky.

A few sweet flow'rets linger still,
  Which Summer left behind;
And still a lingering violet
  Is swaying in the wind.

Once more, I pray thee, love, come out,
  Where happy woodlarks sing,
And dream, while listening to their notes,
  You hear the birds of Spring.

## CHRISTMAS SONG.

Bring the laurel and the bay;
Gather in the holly bright;
Give old Care a holiday;
Let us welcome in delight:
Now for merry-making, play,
Bring the laurel and the bay.

Tell me not of summer flowers
Shedding gladness on the earth,
While we have these smiling hours
Waking winter into mirth.
Tell me not of summer hours;
Love delights in holly bowers.

"Love is come," the cotter sings,
Tuning every heart with joy;
Come, with holy offerings;
Come, in charity's employ;
Blessings in each hand he brings;
"Love is come," the cotter sings.

Christmas comes but once a year—
  Like an angel from above
Cometh the sweet visitor,
  Moving every heart to love;
Rich man with the poor confer,
  Why not have him all the year?

Is there shadow on a brow?
  Is there sorrow at the heart?
Come beneath the holly bough,
  And all sadness will depart.
Joy is there in blossom, now,
Pluck it for thy shaded brow.

Bring the laurel and the bay;
  Bring the holly, sparkling bright;
Ere another Christmas-day
  Cometh, laden with delight,
Many will have passed away,
Where the cypress marks decay.

## MY MOTHER'S BLESSING.

We stood around her dying bed,
  A mournful group, in tears;
And thought of all the words she said
  To us in by-gone years.

A taper flickered in the room,
  And threw its trembling light
Upon the sad and dreary gloom
  That made that solemn night.

We knew the hour was drawing near
  When she from us must part;
Our thought was not an idle fear,
  For death was at her heart.

So there we lingered by her side,
  And watched her, hour by hour;
And once she spoke, before she died,
  With strange unearthly power.

"Why are you weeping, loves, oh why?"
  She asked in gentle tone;
"My peace is made, and God on high
  Has sealed me for His own."

And then she sang the sweetest song
  We ever heard her sing;
"The glory doth to Christ belong,
  My great High Priest and King."

She ceased, when thus I spoke, "My dear,
  Thy hour is almost come;
O bless thy weeping children here,
  Before thou goest home."

She turned upon her bed, and smiled,
  "This blessing, then, be thine,—
Thy day is dark; but hear, my child,
  A brighter sun shall shine."

Again she spoke—a blessed word
  Of cheerfulness she gave;
"My daughters, those who serve the Lord
  Will find a peaceful grave.

"And you, my faithful partner, come!
 Dear husband, pray draw near;
I know how sad will be thy home—
 Here, love, is one more tear."

"There is my brother, too," said I,
 "Who went beyond the sea—
O speak once more before you die."
 "My blessing give," said she.

And ere those words had died away
 Upon the midnight air,
She passed into the realms of day,
 And left us weeping there.

## TO W. F. ROCK, ESQ.,

### ON HIS BIRTH-DAY.

A HAPPY, happy, happy day
May thy to-morrow be.
So friendship sends a cheerful ray
Of light and love for thee.

O, richer than the miser's hoard
Of treasure brought from Ind',
Is the love-knot of golden cord
Which binds thee to thy kind.

And the rich blessing thou hast shed
On others, and on me,
Shall oft return to bless thy head,
As rivers seek the sea.

God bless the group which round thy board
To-morrow morn shall meet,
To render thanks unto the Lord
Before His mercy-seat.

And, 'mid the prayers which shall arise,
  Let my petition sound;
"As stepping-stones to reach the skies,
  May all thy years be found."

## THE PLEASURES OF FANCY.

I AM honest and happy, if not very wise,
With truth in my heart, and love in my eyes;
And those who best know me, proclaim me a bland
And jolly good fellow to shake by the hand.

I am not a boaster, can that be denied?
I've nothing of vanity, plenty of pride;
I am wealthy, aye even when straitened for cash,
But my wealth is not made up of trinkets and trash.

I am not contented, but thankful, I think;
My wishes and wants down to simples will sink;
I've a cottage to live in, a garment to wear,
A crust for my dear ones, and something to spare.

Then why should I envy the lot of a king?
God help him to bear what a kingdom must bring;
And as for a nobleman, 'faith, on my word,
A postman is born just as rich as "my Lord."

Just look at the babe, if the fact you deny;
Now, was he not born just as shoeless as I?
And as for his riches—why, I am a slave
If the chances are not that they make him a knave.

But I, as a Saxon, must think of *his* blood;
That baby, they say, is a Normandy bud;
He has head, hands, and feet, he has fingers and toes,
But his mark of distinction is seen in his nose.

'Tis true, if his fate lends him money and power,
He struts on mortality's stage for an hour;
He eats, drinks, and sleeps, then he yields up his
breath,
And needs his six feet of land after his death.

My Lord keeps a butler to walk in his shoes,
Who hints to his tradesmen to "pluck the old
goose;"
John lives on the best of his beef; and his wine,
Who drinks it?—but that is no business of mine.

I said I was rich—I'm as rich as a Jew!
My treasures are fancies, and precious ones, too.
No matter the part I am called on to play,
I am up to his Lordship, for what he will say.

If trudging through muck is his Lordship's delight,
I'll beat him at that, for a crown or a mite;
Or if he's a notion for leaping a stile,
And he beats me there, then I'll run him a mile.

Is his Lordship "a shot?" I am fond of the fun—
My pouch is my flask, my staff is my gun;
And for velvet, or fustian, or good corduroy,
Hat, gaiters, and boots, I will challenge the boy.

He shoots at a pheasant, I aim at a thrush;
He brings down his game, mine sings in the bush;
His serves for a dinner, but mine, in the spring,
Will perch on the tree-top and merrily sing.

He goes out a fishing, and wanders away,
Where red-spotted trout, and king-fishers play;
He seeks the cold shade with his rod and his line,
And soon I imagine I'm sporting with mine.

Or does he like hunting, and rides with the squire
O'er hedges and ditches bespattered with mire;
Whenever I see the bright scarlet coats pass,
I follow the hounds with my horn and my ass.

He pays for his sporting, his powder, and shot,
And sometimes the game makes a part of my lot;
His pride is to knock down the hare as she starts,
But mine is the pleasure of shooting young hearts.

Then dwell with me, Fancy, for ever, I pray;
The joy of my spirit, the life of my lay:
And I, at thy bidding, will mount on the wing,
Or walk through creation, as proud as a king.

## A DEVONSHIRE PICTURE.

As bright as any morn in June
    Appeared the April sky,
The sea-gull floated 'neath the moon,
    And larks were climbing high.

The gladdie on an hawthorn twig
    His golden vest displayed,
The robin on a higher sprig
    His well-known warble made.

The young rooks on a neighbouring bough
    Were clamouring for food,
The old rooks following the plough
    Were busy for their brood.

The cuckoo singing everywhere
    Made music with the dove,
A lonely swallow winged the air,
    And magpies chattered love.

Above, below, on either side,
Where'er I turned my eye,
Fair Nature seemed a new-made bride,
In love and ecstacy.

As clear as crystal ran the streams,
And peaceful as the hours,
And rapt existence passed in dreams
Upon a couch of flowers.

The bugle reared its purple spire
Beneath the budding broom,
The campion with its star of fire
Was burning into bloom.

Young white-frocked stichworts waved above
The cracky's mossy nest,
Rejoicing where the pixy glove
Will soon hang out its crest.

The wind-flower trembled by the sloe,
As every zephyr flew,
Where ale-hoof and the borage, too,
Held forth their gems of blue.

While, wafted from the cherry-tree,
An odour spread around,
Where spurgewort and dog-mercury
And cuckoo-flowers were found.

That favourite of the butterfly
With primrose-coloured wing,
The dandelion met my eye,
Whose charms few poets sing.

The yellow nettle, thickly set
With buttons round and pale,
And many a shepherd's purse I met
That day along the vale.

Beside the furze-blooth on the hill,
The crowtoe down below,
The yarrow and the robert's-bill,
Full many more I saw.

Hedge-garlic, charlock, scurvy-grass,
Wall-cress and colts-foot gold,
And in a scented woodland pass
Four violets I told.

Sweet woodruff with its tender flower,
    And sorrel's fairy sprite,
That star, too, of the golden hour
    I name the Spring's delight.

The year's first rose, wild strawberry,
    Pea, daisy, perriwink,
Priest Arum, and her Majesty
    Queen Orchis, robed in pink.

A little fancy filled my head,
    As in my hand I took
The orchis from her silken bed,
    In that delightful nook:

I thought a bard, some April hour,
    Had wandered there to think,
And writing something on the flower,
    Had stained its leaves with ink.

Nor shall that pretty blue-eyed gem
    Of lovers be forgot:
I saw the purple budding stem
    Of fair forget-me-not.

## KITTY LILE; OR, MAZED KATE OF CLOVELLY.

UNDER the cliff by the western shore
Wandering ever went she,
Looking for one she will never see more,
In the little cove down by the sea.
When the rock-fowl dropped from their granite homes
To prey on the brit below,
As thickly as bees in their honeycombs,
And white as the driven snow;
And red-winged trawlers flew out of the bay,
Like birds o'er the rainbow sea,
To sport where the fluttering sea-gulls play,
None happier were than she.

Weaving the net by her storm-rocked home,
With hands by the sun embrowned,
And smiling upon the curling foam
That broke on the shell-strewn ground.

She sat 'mid the wave-washed boulders bare,
Thrown up by the tumbling main,
Singing a song to an olden air,
And this was the sweet refrain :—
" My Billy is out with his boat in the bay,
To snare the bright herring for me,
And I, with my arms, in the dimmit of day,
Will snare the bold son of the sea."

Wearily wore one long dark night,
Which followed a threatening eve,
The men in the boats saw the tiny light
That flickered 'neath Katie's eave.
Many, oh many a time she rose,
And looked from her cabin door;
But, grief of griefs, and woe of woes,
The fisher came home no more!
That night, instead of the sweet refrain,
There went forth the bitterest wail,
" My Billy! my Billy!" again and again,
She shrieked to the bellowing gale.

Long, Katie, with look all woe-begone,
Was seen on the little pier,

With a scarlet rag; and her monotone
Fell sad on the stranger's ear.
And when the season for fishing would come,
She waved it down by the sea,
"A token of love he gave her," say some,
"The flag of his own 'Bonny Bee.'"
And ever till death the sweet refrain
She mournfully sang to the wave,
But little wot she that the murmuring main
Was Billy her fisher-boy's grave.

## THE POWER OF SONG.

Who said there was no power in song,
And named it empty sound?
Let but the lash of human wrong
The poet's spirit wound,
And fierce as lightning from the cloud
Shall flash his glance of fire,
And words of might, as thunder loud,
Shall speak his burning ire.

Ye talk of deeds; say, what is *thought*,
When marching through a line,
When with a potent grandeur fraught,
And harmony divine?
Doth it not seize upon the soul,
And bear it far away,
As ships which on the ocean roll,
By winds are driven? Say!

Hath it not shone a glorious light
Where all was dark before,
And blest the sons of toil with might
To win a distant shore?
And hath not error fled from truth,
And tyranny been hurled
By poets from its throne of ruth,
The grim curse of the world?

Then say not song is void of power;
It melts the negro's chains;
No bird in love's enchanting bower
Can sing such pleasant strains.
A giant in the cause of right;
The harbinger of fame;
It nerves the warrior for the fight,
And gilds the victor's name.

## THE BLACKBERRY GIRL.

I SAW her like the virgin moon,
  A beauty half in shade,
The angel of some poet's dream,
  The spirit of the glade.
Her voice was sweeter than the brook
  That warbled through the dale,
And every linnet came to woo
  The maid of Cherry Vale.

Alone within a coppice sat
  The gentle maiden shy;
Her carpet was the curly moss,
  Her palace-roof the sky.
The bloom upon her bonny cheek
  Made e'en the blush-rose pale,
As sunshine through the branches kissed
  The flower of Cherry Vale.

A slender sapling, lowly bent,
  Made her leaf-woven seat;

And like a nymph fair Annie looked,
  Within her green retreat.
A crown of lady-fern she wore,
  Which, shaken by the gale,
Threw softly trembling shadows o'er
  The rose of Cherry Vale.

The vermeil-beaded bryony,
  In many a graceful wind,
Hung dangling from her swan-white neck,
  And round her arms entwined.
Her eyes, twin stars stolen from the night,
  Told a bewitching tale,
How Love had gently wooed and won
  The maid of Cherry Vale.

O, why is life a weary way
  Of heavy toil and pain?
Health laughs on every breezy hill,
  And joy on every plain.
Go cull, like her, the luscious gem
  Where English brambles trail,
And bloom like Nature's favourite,
  The flower of Cherry Vale.

## "WOODLANDS."

I KNOW a cottage perched upon a hill;
A sylvan home, a nest among the trees,
Where oft the clatter of a neighbouring mill
Goes murmuring up upon the friendly breeze;
In sooth, so rural is that lovely cot,
The wind, the mill, and ringing anvil's clink,
And fisher's song beside the river's brink,
And ploughboy's whistle, and the lime-team's trot,
And milkmaid's carol o'er her luscious drink,
Are the chief sounds that reach that blissful spot:

Save when the linnets' chorus streameth down,
And bleating flocks and cattle wake the lea,
When thrushes warble in the elm tree's crown,
And skylarks, through dense showers of harmony,
Mount up, and soar above the happy throngs,
To sport awhile among the cloudlets white;—
What joy! to hear them in their circling flight,
Trilling their love-notes with their merry tongues,
Paving their pathways with their own sweet songs;
Birds spurning earth, air-birds, and winged with light.

It sits so high, that ere the Yeo, a stream
  That stealeth by it, creeping to the sea,
Is lighted with the virgin morning's beam,
  Its windows sparkle bright and silverly;
Not only does it win the earliest kiss
  Of sunny morning's sweet and rosy mouth,
But all the balmy odours of the south
  Conspire to make it one dear scene of bliss;
No accent there is heard of speech uncouth,
  Nor do its inmates one pure pleasure miss.

There is a pathway winding up the steep,
  O'erhung with chestnut-bloom and sycamore,
The woodbines there in forms fantastic creep,
  And primrose tufts and mosses strew the floor;
The thorn blows there, and holly overgrown
  With ivy, bearing many-shapen leaves,
Which some sweet wood-nymph in the noontide weaves,
  Or when the Night her mantle dark has thrown
Over the gold and purple of the eves,
  Or at the twilight of the infant dawn.

The clematis, the sorrel, and wild brier,
  Wood-briony, and brambles, flourish there;

There summer zephyrs fan the poppy's fire,
  And heath, and gorse, and dog-rose scent the air.
A shelter from the cold North's biting wind,
  The partridge seeks its broad and sunny glade,
The pheasant lodges in its ample shade;
  And pies, the robbers of the feathery kind,
Th' aërial homes of squirrels oft invade,
  And there the bees their sweetest blossoms find.

O blest retreat, green haunt of poesy,
  There I could dwell a studious solitaire,
And, nestled in thy bower of melody,
  Forego the pleasures which the world deems rare.
I only ask to see the spreading dale
  That sleeps below thy bristling, pine-girt base,
To hear the horn and view the lively chase,
  And watch the sea-gull ride upon the gale;
Or mark the leaping of the silver dace
  In Tor's bright waters dancing down the vale.

There I would meditate on days gone by,
  When Monk for Stuart played his famous part,
With peaceful Landcross present to my eye,
  The birth-place of that brave old warrior-heart.

But let me sing some softer, sweeter theme,
Bright home of beauty, and the fondest loves!
Young Edward often in his midnight dream
Revisits thee beneath the May-moon's beam,
To list the cooing of thy native doves,
For Bessie then most beautiful doth seem.

I will not dwell on Anne and charming Kate,
The first a rose, the last a lily fair,
Or wish the angels had an earthly mate,
Their virtues are so heavenly, and so rare!
It were almost a sin to wish it so;
But Bessie, lovelier than an angel, she
Hath clothed herself in our humanity,
To walk the earth a spirit robed in snow,
And give her Edward her society,
And teach us sinners purity below.

I heard her once, 'twas when the bright-eyed June
Was shooting down her arrows through the trees,
And ever since, like some sweet, soothing tune,
Her voice I hear in every flitting breeze.

It was so mellow, like the fall of dew;
  And then her cheeks, made fresher by the sun,
Blushed out with such a warm and roseate tone,
  I thought 'twas Eve to Eden come anew,
As down the checkered path she tripped alone,
  And almost worshiping, I sighed adieu!

Thrice happy cot, if there the bard should stray
  By some kind chance, and rap-tap at its door,
In bleak December or in blooming May,
  He always finds it open to the poor.
"Come in! come in!" the hearty sire exclaims;
  And then the matron, smiling, meets her guest,
With modest Ellen blushing to the breast,
  And stately Carrie, with her queen of names,
And gentle Agnes, lovely as the rest;
  Each one a grace and sharing equal claims.

Heaven bless thee, "Woodlands," joy be with the
    girls!
  And summers ever smiling in their eyes,
And their luxuriant drops of flowing curls,
  The only clouds that shadow o'er their skies!

And soon may Edward, with his form erect,
  And raven eyes and locks of glossy jet,
His mother's promise and the maiden's pride,
  In thy blest pathways, smiling, be descried,
Culling for Bessie, bell and violet,
  To grace the bosom of his new-made bride.

## SONG OF THE LITTLEHAM HOP-PICKERS.

When the leaf is turning brown,
And the year is nine moons old,
A merry group we gambol down
To our bowers of green and gold;
And there, like the birds that sing
In the broad and branchy tree,
We make the moss-floored woodlands ring,
To "Merry hop-pickers are we."

CHORUS.

Then come where the hop-vines blow,
And trout-streams wander free,
When orchards wear their golden glow,
And join in the hop-girls' glee.

As the morning sunlight gleams,
We hie to our garden dell,
And coax our lads from their sleek-backed teams
To toy with the bright hop bell;

And wreathing our brows with the flowers,
  And taxing our lips for their fee,
Our days dance by like summer hours,
  To "Merry hop-pickers are we."

Then come where the hop-vines blow,
  And trout-streams wander free,
When orchards wear their golden glow,
  And join in the hop-girls' glee.

## STREW THE ROSES.

### A MARRIAGE SONG.

STREW the roses, quaff the wine,
  Fill the golden cup of joy,
Bring the orange and the vine,
  Let the lily find employ;
Love is come to Hymen's shrine,
  Strew the roses, quaff the wine.

## A THOUGHT AMONG THE FLOWERS.

LIVING on the sunlight, drinking in the rain,
Dying in the winter time, springing up again,
Bringing, in your honey-bud, nectar for the bee;
O my little floweret, thou art a mystery.
Living on the sunlight, drinking in the rain,
Dying in the winter time, springing up again,
Springing in our little ones, flowerets like you;
O my little violet, we are a mystery too.

## THE LASS OF WATERTOWN.

O! the bonny, bonny Yeo;
O, the silver-crested Yeo,
With daffodil and primrose banks,
And meadows pranked with snow;
There the mavis sits at noon,
To hear its native tune,
And learn the mellowed music
Of its wavelets, as they flow.

There 's a rustic rose-bound cot,
On a sweetly rural spot,
Like a lovely milk-white lily,
On its ripples looking down.
And the rarest treasure there,
Is my pretty Polly fair;
My laughing blue-eyed Polly,
The Lass of Watertown.

When the Eve, in purple drest,
With her one star on her breast,

Leads up the young and modest Moon,
To see her sire lie down;
Or when the jewelled Night
Gives out her smiles of light,
I love to pace its margin,
With the Lass of Watertown.

Whilst the mills upon its bank,
With their busy din and clank,
And roar of rushing torrents,
All other clamours drown,
With the bird upon the bough,
I breathe my twilight vow,
And mark the sweet confusion
Of the Lass of Watertown.

O! the bonny, bonny Yeo;
Where the hawthorns hanging low,
Spread a fragrant sun-screen, woven,
And overlaid with down;
Where the sleek and dappled kine
Breathe an odour like the vine;
There for ever I would wander,
With the Lass of Watertown.

Flow gently, softly flow,
Let thy waters murmur low,
For my loved one is departed,
My beauty and my crown!
And nightly by thy side
I will watch thy loving tide:
Leap up to kiss my darling,
The Lass of Watertown.

Flow faster, faster flow,
My bright and bonny Yeo,
And help to swell the chorus,
As thy waters gambol down;
Until the song is heard
From maiden, man, and bird,
O! come again, sweet Polly,
Fair Lass of Watertown.

## TAKE THY HARP, CHORISTER!

Take thy harp, Chorister!
  Passion is glowing;
Strike while my song
  In its fervour is flowing;
Strike for the peoples
  Their freedom desiring;
Strike, for bold music
  Is ever inspiring.

Hark to the patriot,
  In his cell praying,
"Sheathe thy sword, Warrior!
  Purpled with slaying,
Faith in all human right
  Fails at its fountain;
Strike thy harp, Chorister,
  Bard of the mountain!"

Take thy harp, Chorister!
  Nations are crying;
Strike for the prison-bound,
  Bleeding and dying;
Strike it for Liberty,
  Now and hereafter;
Strike, till the world changes
  Weeping for laughter.

## CARRIE DENE.

LILY-BROWED and rosy-cheeked,
Sprightly as a hare,
Cherry-lipped and azure-eyed,
Innocent and fair,
Dimple-chinned and golden-locked,
Stately as a queen,
Pride of all the villagers
Was my Carrie Dene.

Where a little foot-way bridge
Spans a silver stream,
Pictured on the running wave
Like a rosy dream,
There I first beheld the maid,
Dressed in cottage-green;
And when I would help her o'er,
"No," said Carrie Dene.

As my Carrie threw on me
  Her bewitching eye,
Love, in trembling eloquence,
  Told her with a sigh—
'There is no one on the earth
  Fair as you, I ween,'
And on wings of joy I flew
  And kissed my Carrie Dene.

Often at the twilight hour,
  Dressed in cottage-green,
As I met her on the bridge,
  Comes my Carrie Dene,
Telling me how Love befooled,
  And chained her to the scene,
Else she ne'er had changed the name
  Of pretty Carrie Dene.

## TO THE HONOURABLE MARK ROLLE,

### ON HIS COMING OF AGE.

Too much before the golden calf as suppliants we bow,
And sacrifice at Mammon's shrine the virtue and the vow.
Not such an one is he who doth this honest prayer indite,
"God help thee like a man to choose the noble and the right."
List! hear the Exe rejoicing as she runs toward the sea;
From the womb of yonder moorland comes the lovely and the free,
And the thousand tiny rivulets which creep by fern and flower
She hath twisted into unity, a beauty and a power.

So gather up thy energies, and live with every breath,
And walk the earth a child of strength, and love, outliving death;
The Present make thy fulcrum, let the Past thy lever be,
And the Future—aye, the FUTURE—shall rise glorious to thee!

In the silence of the study, at meditation's hour,
Thou hast learnt the use of riches, and the great design of power;
That kings are light as bubbles when weighed against a breath,
And wealth is but a bauble thing when face to face with death.
Thou hast crossed the ancient threshold of the grand and solemn past,
And wandered 'mid the ruins of its cities famed and vast;
Thou hast heard old Jacob speaking from Egypt's sandy plain,
And the voice of the Messiah from Zion's sacred fane;

Thou hast stood where yellow Tiber its dirge-like anthem sings,
And amid the shades of Athens, and graves of buried kings,
The Spartan's voice hath reached thee from his tomb among the weeds;
And the Future is thy heritage,—go, crown it with thy deeds.

## POCKET FRIENDS.

When the soul is out of tune,
    Leave the bitter paths of strife,
With Nature to commune,
    And share her quiet life:
Go, wander on the hill,
Or track some winding rill,
With a minstrel in your pocket,
    To carol to your wife.

Sometimes it may be Keats,
    All the better if 'tis May,
To bear his dainty sweets
    Like a posy on the way.
Better still if it is June,
For the music of his tune
Will give a sweeter meaning
    To what the linnets say.

In the narrow village road,
    'Mid cottages and flowers,
With observation broad,
    Would you pass your leisure hours?
Let Wordsworth be your guide,
And the old man in his pride
Will make you feel the beauty
    Of his philosophic powers.

With Hood you weep and smile,
    And Shelley is a joy;
Poor Clare will woe beguile,
    Or Giles, the "Farmer's Boy;"
While Thomson ever brings
With Coleridge pleasant things,
And Goldsmith, ever loving,
    Will always bring employ.

Would you list the sound of mirth,
    As you wander 'mid the ferns;
Would you joy around the hearth,
    Shake the hearty hand of Burns;

Or halt beside the brook,
To hear Eliza Cook
Pipe out a merry solo,
    Which all the nation learns.

Quaint Chaucer, ever young,
    And Spenser—Nature's twain—
Old Herrick with his song,
    And glorious "Rare old Ben,"
Leigh Hunt, who loves the sward,
And Moore, green Erin's bard,
On mountain, mead, or moorland,
    Are the merriest of men.

If in deep poetic mood,
    And lonely you would be,
Let your study be the wood,
    And thought your company.
Then wave your fancy's wand,
And presently shall stand,
The bard of "In Memoriam,"
    To light and counsel thee.

Perchance among the boughs
 Of the grandly solemn trees,
Like softly whispered vows
 Of lovers on the breeze,
You may hear a gentle voice,
If Cowper is your choice,
Till your solitude grows vocal
 With pleasant harmonies.

The din of distant war
 Through the silence you may hear;
And the battle is not far,
 If you have Campbell near.
And over classic Greece
You may throw a glance in peace,
And sing the great are fallen
 To Byron's sad guitar.

If imagination plays,
 And you fly upon its wings,
To those old imperial days,
 Which mighty Homer sings;

With Landor seek to rove,
Through some academic grove,
And the grey-browed sage will utter
  Strange long-forgotten things.

There is majesty sublime
  In Milton's glorious song,
And thoughts for every time
  As Shakespeare strides along:
Brave-hearted, high-souled man,
Though last, he leads the van,
And Nature cries "Behold him!"
  With never-ceasing tongue.

## SPRING.

O Spring, bright Spring, season of birds and flowers,
Life, fragrance, song, and beauty;
Delight is born from thy young hours,
To prattle in thy budding bowers,
Sweeter than bells in ivied towers,
When doing merry duty.

## THE RIVER.

From its sedge-lipped fountain flowing,
Down the hill-side, through the vale,
By the cottage, meadow, orchard,
Telling one delightful tale.
Dimpling, whirling, dancing, purling,
Sweetly babbling in its course;
Bright and happy, wandering minstrel,
Singing of its native source.
God the fount, and Love the river,
Even so our life should be,
Ever blessing, praising ever,
One perpetual melody.

## THE SWALLOWS' MATIN.

WHILE up on high the sky-lark soars to sing,
  Linnets and finches carol on the spray,
  On garden-gate the robin pipes his lay,
And cuckoos give soft music on the wing;
The thrush proclaims the advent of the spring
From the green umbrage of new budding leaves;
The friendly swallows from our cottage eaves
  Tune the dim moments of the dubious day.
I love those watchers for the rising sun,
  Whose cheerful work is to salute the morn
Before the blackbird's carol is begun,
  Or ere the dew has washed his golden horn:
Let but those minstrels give their morning glee,
And I, contented, Sleep, can part with thee.

## THE HOLY HOUR.

METHOUGHT the clouds kept Sabbath—and the calm
That settled on me, soft as summer-balm,
Was like the silence sleeping 'mid the hills,
And only broken by the mountain rills.
Or you may liken it unto the hush
Of eventide, before the songs of thrush
And other warblers tune the darkening air;
The stillness 'twixt the chime and morning prayer,
Before the organ's grand and solemn peal
Roars through the trembling aisles; before we kneel
As suppliants at the sacred throne of grace,
Meek mercy-seekers in the holy place.
Calm as the gentle break of morning light,
The moon, white-breasted, brooding on the night,
Whilst many-handed Industry lay still,
And Peace sat throned upon her purple hill.

## THE BATTLE OF THOUGHT.

AYE, past is the era of chivalrous glory,
  Forgotten its hero may rest in his tomb,
Since scarce will the deed high emblazoned in story
  Fetch a thrill of response from the bosom of home.
For a warfare more righteous than crusade is raging,
  Its foe is Oppression, with beauty 'tis fraught;
'Tis the light of the soul with its darkness engaging,
  And the battle we fight is the Battle of Thought.

On Error's dark field see old Folly lies bleeding,
  And pompous-puffed Bigots no longer are brave,
For heroes of mind through ill habits are leading,
  And soon o'er the passions their standard shall wave.
The sensual man seeks a loftier station—
  He prizes his birthright, it cannot be bought—
He takes his true stand on his God's wide creation,
  For the battle we fight is the Battle of Thought.

Hark! Peace, with her silver-tongued trumpet is
sounding,
See Justice attends her with Reason and Care;
Whilst Science and Art on light tip-toe are bounding,
And Truth, armed with Literature, brings up the rear.
On, then, champions, on, never think of retreating,
Let "love" be your watchword, and wisdom be
taught;
And victors you must be, all rebels defeating,
Who serve in our battle, the Battle of Thought.

We blame not the hero, the patriot toiling,
Who fell in his fighting, disdaining to flee.
For the aim of his life was the perfect despoiling
The despots of thought, that the soul might be free.
We'll crown our brave Nelsons with laurels unfading;
We yield royal Cambridge the honours he sought;
They baffled the scheme of the foemen invading,
And battled for home, and the freedom of Thought.

They gallantly rode o'er the white-crested billow,
Nor cared if the sea or the sod made their grave,
Well knowing their country, in cypress and willow,
Would mourn their true worth o'er the tombs of
the brave.

They battled for Peace—'twas a noble vocation;
They crushed the proud foe, who for rapine had fought;
And long shall they live in the heart of their nation,
For Britons can breathe the pure current of Thought.

## AUTUMN BERRIES.

Daughters of the Autumn, beautiful are ye,
Blushing on the dog-rose and the holly tree;
Burning on the hawthorn, flaming through the sedge,
Where the honeysuckle creeps up the hazel hedge,
Twisting, twining, brightly shining,
Ever with a joyful face,
Like a maiden, jewel laden,
Clinging with a fond embrace.

Children of the Autumn, richer far are ye
Than the ruddy coraline underneath the sea;
Rich as the cornelian, with its ruby sheen,
Is the red ox-berry wreath round the bramble seen,
Twisting, twining, ever shining,
Smiling like a rosy boy;
Much I love ye, far above me,
Glancing from your haunts so coy.

Berries of the Autumn, maidens make of ye
Pretty crimson ear-drops—from the guelder tree
Necklaces the children of your scarlet beads
Make, and ruby-bright coronas for their little heads.
Twisting, twining, ever shining,
Bygone days ye bring to mind—
When my sister crowned, I kissed her—
Days in memory e'er enshrined.

Monarch of the Autumn, what a mellowed hue
Hath thy bell, vermilioned, melancholy yew?
While the mountain-ash fruit, and Canterbury thorn,
Rival the warm blushes of the virgin morn.
Beauty-blushing, glory-gushing,
Deeper than the sun-set dyes;
Scarlet-streaming, passion-gleaming,
To the Poet's loving eyes.

Sing a song for Autumn, month of mirth and play,
Sing it in the orchard, wheresoe'er you stray;
While children cull the diamonds which on the brambles shine,

And hedges yield the poor-man's-grapes which make his elder wine.

Rich as cherries are ye, berries,
On the bryony and rose;
But the bramble, as we ramble,
With the brightest lustre glows.

## EDGAR AND EDITH.

### A FOREST SCENE.

*Edgar.*—Bonny maid, come dwell with me,
Where the wild dogs burrow and the deer roam free;
And I'll kill for thee the kid, and the younglings of the kine,
And milk shall be thy drink, and the sweet juice of the vine.
Adown in hollow vales, where wood-birds sing,
Twanging the yew-bow we'll pass the spring;
We'll sleep away the golden days, we'll laugh away the brown,
And a winter couch I'll make thee of the wild-swan's down.
Wilt go with me?

*Edith.*— Aye, love, with thee;
And we'll nestle like young doves
When the night comes down.

And as mist upon the meadows
In the morn shall be thy shadows,
My joy, my own beloved,
    My glory and my crown.

*Edgar.*—More lovely than the blossom
    On the white-thorn tree,
And sweeter than the honey
    Is my love to me.
As we wander by the river
I will sing of thee for ever.
My love shall be my song-bird,
    My love shall be my sun;
I'll name thee, bonny June,
I'll ask no other moon,
And our hearts shall beat together
    Henceforth as they were one.
Heigho, heigho, come let us go,
And twang the bow
    Till the night comes down.

*Edith.*—And as the days shall fade
    I'll sit in yonder glade.

*Edgar.*—A Queen among the violets.

*Edith.*—And watch thee weave thy fowling nets,
    Where the old oaks frown.

## COME LIST, MY LOVE.

Come list, my love, and I will sing
A song O, a song O.
Come list, my love, and I will sing,
Of all the seasons give me spring,
For youth and beauty it doth bring,
And joy O, and joy O.

The bud half blown, my love, for me,
For aye O, for aye O.
The bud half blown, my love, for me,
The maiden bark upon the sea,
The young bird singing on the tree,
For aye O, for aye O.

The morn, with dew upon its head,
For me O, for me O.
The morn, with dew upon its head,
The sun new rising from his bed,
The first love of a gentle maid,
And thine O, and thine O.

## TO BESSY.

I never more thy face may see,
Thou little smiling elf;
Yet thou, sweet child, must ever be
A portion of myself.

Within the memory's sacred hall
Thy lovely form shall live,
Like painting on a pictured wall,
And purest pleasure give.

And if despair comes haunting me,
Upon life's mortal plain,
I'll make an angel-child of thee,
To bid me hope again.

Thou little bud of beauty rare,
Right joyous be thy lot,
A life-time like the summer fair,
My bonny, bright-eyed dot.

## LYNTON.

'Twas when the purple evening painted heaven,
And day declining sought a place to die,
Sojourning in the Switzerland of Devon,
I wandered out beneath its twi-lit sky;
Around the north walk strolled my friend and I,
And gazed with wonder from our dizzy height.
Beneath us roared the sea, and far on high
Rude rocks hung threatening, and might well affright.
It seeméd much as we went on our way,
Eyeing the toppling ivy-mantled pile,
That Nature on that spot had ceased to smile,
And earth itself was tumbling to decay.
Nought saw we in that evening's dusky gray,
But one lone sheep, which wondering fled away.

## THE VALLEY OF ROCKS.

WILD vale of rocks, stern monument sublime
Of Power Almighty, here the hoary sage
Long walked and worshipped in the morn of time,
Nor needed he the aid of lettered page
To speak of God in that primæval age.
Those forms grotesque that crown the seaward steep,
The gloom, the silence which the waste doth keep,
The thunder's voice, and the hoarse tempest's rage,
The Druid filled with reverential awe.
O, wilderness of echoes! when the moon
Lifted her crescent on that night of June,
And threw her weird light on the rocks below,
I and my friend, with solemn words and slow,
Thanked God one tiny star-worm there did glow.

## THE FUNERAL AT THE MANSION.

LET history crown the warrior,
For the well-fought fields he trod;
I sing of his peaceful homestead,
His tomb in the "acre of God."

He is gone, and the good year dying
Hath whispered to Autumn sere,
Go bid old white-haired Winter,
Prepare him a shroud for his bier.

Let his broad-sword rust in its scabbard,
A wail be heard for the song,
And the charger that neighs for his rider,
Let him call for him loud and long.

The bell for devotion ringeth,
But one will be missed from the prayer;
He sleeps in an upper chamber,
And Death is the warder there.

All music is hushed in the mansion,
    The timbrel, the harp, and the lute;
The harpist is there—but a mourner;
    The minstrel—but dumb as a mute.

And white blinds hang in the windows,
    And silence holds court in the hall,
No sounds are heard there but death-whispers,
    No story, save that of the pall.

The messenger bringeth his letters,
    But the man of the sword is gone,
And no one inquireth the tidings,
    In the old familiar tone.

And sad is the messenger's spirit,
    As he treads on the porchway floor,
For the house is the tomb of its master,
    And Death hath the key of his door.

The old men weep in the court-yard,
    They weep till their eyes grow red;
They weep, for each poor old servant
    Has lost a friend in the dead.

The hearse is outside the mansion,
    The soldier is borne in his shroud,
Until in the little green churchyard,
    It halts 'midst a gazing crowd.

And now, in the grey-grown temple,
    The coffin, exposed to view,
Shows a plate, with the name of the sleeper,
    To the stranger that sits in his pew.

The minister opens the volume,
    And reads an epistle from Paul;
And the words of the grand old poem
    Give hope to each sorrowing soul.

He is borne to the grave of his fathers;
    And as thither the mourners repair,
The tramp of the bearers and horses
    Beats out the death-march on the air.

He sinks in the grave's deep hollow,
    And close by the empty bier
Crowds many a loving weeper,
    To drop the last sad tear.

## FRIENDSHIP.

Friendship, soothing balm of care,
More than precious, more than rare,
Queen of virtues, every gem
Sparkles in thy diadem.
Every charm in love's employ,
Every pure domestic joy,
Social hours of purest mirth,
Are the children of thy birth.
Every virtue prized by men
Follows in thy royal train,
Tender pity, mercy kind,
Graceful ornaments of mind,
Joined with courage, own thy sway,
Love thy rule, and homage pay.
Not a glory of the skies,
Not a charm that earth supplies,
Not the painter's noblest scene,
Not the poet's song, I ween,

E'er can shadow forth thy worth,
'Tis of so divine a birth.
Yonder orbs that brightly shine,
All their attributes are thine;
Beauty doth encircle thee,
Loveliness and majesty.
Wealth with thee feels richer still;
Poverty, but half its ill:
Give me, spite of nature's store,
Friendship, and I ask no more.
'Tis a sun, whose genial ray
Warms the coldest winter day;
'Tis the moon, whose silvery light
'Luminates the darkest night;
'Tis the seaman's friendly star,
When the winds with ocean war;
'Tis the planet's ceaseless roll,
In the system of the soul;
'Tis the sea whence vapours soar,
High to slake the thirsty shore;
'Tis the stream, which doth again
Bear them to the generous main;
'Tis a rock midst shifting sand;
'Tis a wise magician's wand;

'Tis the old sepulchral yew,
Mingling tears with sacred dew,
Lest the virtues of the dead
Dry like grass upon his bed;
'Tis the bird that wakes the vale,
When all other songsters fail,
Coming early, coming late,
Perching on the garden gate,
Singing, most melodiously,
"Friendship! there is nought like thee!"

## BONNIE McKIEL.

BONNIE McKiel! Bonnie McKiel!
I dinna loe ony but Bonnie McKiel;
Sae couthie and cosie, wi wee lippies rosie,
The pride o' a' lassies is Bonnie McKiel.

Bonnie McKiel! Bonnie McKiel!
The light o' my e'e is Bonnie McKiel;
I wadna gang roaming at a' in the gloaming,
Were it no' for the starnies of Bonnie McKiel.

Bonnie McKiel! Bonnie McKiel!
There 's music enoo in Bonnie McKiel
To make a bard jingle for aye at his ingle,
And burst all his bagpipes for Bonnie McKiel.

Bonnie McKiel! Bonnie McKiel!
She sings like the birdies, sweet Bonnie McKiel;
And all the blue burnies that gang on their journeys
Breathe saftly the praises o' Bonnie McKiel.

Bonnie McKiel! Bonnie McKiel!
I'll tell ye a prixy o' Bonnie McKiel:
I kenned that she loed me, and if she had wooed me,
I wad na loe less my own Bonnie McKiel.

Bonnie McKiel! Bonnie McKiel!
She cam' o'er the brig ane night fra the mill,
And crooning told Maggie that Donald McCraiggie
Was just the young laddie for Bonnie McKiel.

Bonnie McKiel! Bonnie McKiel!
Get up in the stairs noo, Bonnie McKiel,
For hame comes the laddie alang wi his daddie,
I'll spak o' his wooing sweet Bonnie McKiel.

Bonnie McKiel! Bonnie McKiel!
The lassie that lives just awa at the mill;
She 's blithe, and the miller has plenty o' siller;
Gude faith! she would suit thee, young Bonnie McKiel.

Bonnie McKiel! Bonnie McKiel!
I swore I wad dee for the maid o' the mill;
Sae then we gang'd trysting where bindweeds loe twisting,
And noo I am happy wi' Bonnie McKiel.

## THE LIFE-BOAT VOLUNTEER.

All snugly in his berth on shore an old tar lay,
Like a norwester snoring,
And dreamt he lived o'er many a day,
When he went out exploring;
Of the wreck on the ice, and the dainty slice
His shipmates won from his body twice,
Which the lot made them buy at a famine price.
The washings and dashings,
The smashings and crashings,
The jars and wars, the raft made of spars,
The watch on the deck, and the course by the stars.
The storms he had braved,
And the lads he had saved;
The girls he had loved in the ports he had entered,
And the one whom to win he had everything ventured.
Yes, years ago, he had loved her so,
There was nought for her sake but he'd suffer or do.

Ay, he used to say, if down he should go,
He would call at the first grog-shop below,
And when he'd a glass of the very best,
He'd place his hand on his honest old breast,
And swear he would never forget her.

Yet, all this time, a storm raged high,
And a ship had struck 'neath a starless sky;
While the wild winds sang with a furious clang,
The bell on the deck repeatedly rang,
And the minute-gun boomed out a solemn bang.
Still, strange to say, while the tempest rung,
He snoring lay in blanket bay,
And thought in his hammock aboard he swung.
But now, 'mid the roar of the surf-fringed shore,
A well-known voice he heard:
"There 's a wreck in the bay, Hurray, boys, Hurray!"
And the old tar woke at the word.
"The life-boat, the life-boat, Hurray, boys, Hurray!
How the old house rocks with the gale!"
"Come, come, boy, rouse up, there's a wreck in the bay!"
"Where? where?" "On the northermost tail."
"By Joe, 'tis a sneezer; by heaven, it blows,
I'll be there in a jiffey, my lad;

We'll save them, my boys, from old Davy's white jaws,
Good heavens! the breakers are mad.
    Here 's the tight little craft, boys,
    Come, haul her, boys, haul!
    Show her nose to the sea, boys,
    She'll weather the squall.
Here 's go for the first, to pull or to steer,
That's right, lads, jump in—don't delay;
Ten pressed men can't weather a brave volunteer;
Pull hard, boys—Hurray, boys, Hurray!"
"Hurray! Hurray!" the landsmen shout.
    "Hurray! Hurray! Hurray!
She sails like a Mur on the mountain wave,
And dips like a drake in the sea.
Pull, lads, pull, ye 're a sturdy crew;
    As ever dipped oar in a wave.
Hurrah! for the lads in the tight 'True Blue,'
    For they go the lost to save."
"Hold on, boys; back-water. Come, one pull more!
Hold hard, boys; look out for the rope!
Come, cheer up, drop handsome, we'll save you; that's
        right;
Sit fast there—be manly and hope.
Let go now; be gentle, she weathers it well;

Pull hard, boys; come, pull with your might!
Be steady; here comes a great shark of a swell;
Three cheers, boys! Hurray, boys! All right!
Cheerly boys, Ho! on we go, steady and slow;
Cheerly, boys, Ho! Ho! Ho! Ho! Ho! Cheerly,
boys, Ho!
Hurrah! Hurrah! Hurrah!"

J. UNWIN, GRESHAM STEAM PRESS, BUCKLERSBURY, LONDON.

CPSIA information can be obtained
at www.ICGtesting.com
Printed in the USA
LVHW030637230223
740173LV00002B/66